A brilliant glint sparkled between his lips as he curved a sun-shaming smile.

"Wait." Was she hallucinating? She narrowed her gaze against the sunlight. The man was...real? Couldn't be.

"There's not supposed to be anyone on this island." Never had her imagination conjured the real thing.

Her heart stuttered. He didn't look like a serial killer come to claim his next victim.

No. Chill, Saralyn. He was just staff. Or a fisherman who had anchored his boat nearby?

Whoever he was, he was stunning.

And she was a pale middle-aged woman wearing a teeny bikini.

She stood, grasping for her silk scarf, then remembered she'd left it in the villa. Shoot! She clasped her hands across her tummy, where she sported that unasked-for menopausal bulge.

"Who are you?" Body discomfort aside, this wasn't right. "This is my island."

"Is it now?" A bemused smile glinted in the stranger's eyes. Dark irises, probably whiskey brown or even earthen umber. His mouth quirked in a seductive smirk, like a romance hero set to seduce the heroine with his charming aloofness. "Your island?"

T0284391

Dear Reader,

As I'm writing this story, it is winter here in Minnesota. For some reason, when my stories are set in summer, I tend to write them in winter, and vice versa. But what a weird winter, indeed, with sixty-degree temperatures in February! All to say, I guess my longings show up on the page. Who doesn't desire a private tropical island for a "finding myself" getaway? It was great fun getting introverted and burned-by-divorce Saralyn into a bikini and onto a beach, where she relaxed, released all of life's worries and even welcomed her fiftieth birthday. Until... Well, it wouldn't be a very interesting story if she just lounged on the beach alone for two weeks, would it? Cue the sexy hero, David, who is about to turn her whole world upside down.

If you are reading this when the winds are shrill and the snowflakes are falling, I feel you, dear reader. I really do. Here's to diving into our fantasies on the page!

Michele

TWO WEEK TEMPTATION IN PARADISE

MICHELE RENAE

Harlequin

ROMANCE

If you purchased this book without a cover you should be aware that this book is stolen property. It was reported as "unsold and destroyed" to the publisher, and neither the author nor the publisher has received any payment for this "stripped book."

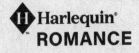

**Harlequin®
ROMANCE**

Recycling programs for this product may not exist in your area.

ISBN-13: 978-1-335-21611-3

Two Week Temptation in Paradise

Copyright © 2024 by Michele Hauf

All rights reserved. No part of this book may be used or reproduced in any manner whatsoever without written permission.

Without limiting the author's and publisher's exclusive rights, any unauthorized use of this publication to train generative artificial intelligence (AI) technologies is expressly prohibited.

This is a work of fiction. Names, characters, places and incidents are either the product of the author's imagination or are used fictitiously. Any resemblance to actual persons, living or dead, businesses, companies, events or locales is entirely coincidental.

For questions and comments about the quality of this book, please contact us at CustomerService@Harlequin.com.

TM and ® are trademarks of Harlequin Enterprises ULC.

 Harlequin Enterprises ULC
22 Adelaide St. West, 41st Floor
Toronto, Ontario M5H 4E3, Canada
www.Harlequin.com

Printed in U.S.A.

Michele Renae is the pseudonym for award-winning author Michele Hauf. She has published over ninety novels in historical, paranormal and contemporary romance and fantasy, as well as written action/adventure as Alex Archer. Instead of "writing what she knows," she prefers to write "what she would love to know and do" (and yes, that includes being a jewel thief and/or a brain surgeon).

You can email Michele at toastfaery@gmail.com.
Instagram: @MicheleHauf
Pinterest: @ToastFaery

Books by Michele Renae

Harlequin Romance

If the Fairy Tale Fits...

Cinderella's Billion-Dollar Invitation

Cinderella's Second Chance in Paris
The CEO and the Single Dad
Parisian Escape with the Billionaire
Consequence of Their Parisian Night

Visit the Author Profile page at Harlequin.com.

Happy birthday to you! You look marvelous.
You shine. And I'm so glad you are in this world!

Praise for
Michele Renae

"Renae's debut Harlequin [Romance] novel
is a later-in-life romance that's sure to tug
at readers' heartstrings."

—*Library Journal* on
Cinderella's Second Chance in Paris

CHAPTER ONE

SARALYN MARTIN HAD not worn a bikini in twenty years.

The dressing room she stood in was attached to a luxurious bedroom that boasted a king-size bed, all-natural linens and floor-to-ceiling windows that overlooked a white sand beach frilled with emerald palm trees. Luxurious island getaway for one? Check!

With a discerning eye she studied her reflection. Having lived in California the past two decades, she owned many swimsuits, all of them a one-piece. The coverage boosted her oft-lacking self-confidence. Yet, she was here to shake up her life. Step out of her comfort zone. Become a new woman! Bikinis had been the logical choice for this two-week vacation and she intended to wear them daily.

Sucking in her tummy, she prodded at her hips. Bit more flesh there than she'd prefer, but as she faced her fiftieth birthday wearing the new crown of menopause, wasn't she allowed some padding?

Not by Hollywood standards. Fortunately, she no longer claimed Hollywood-wife status.

A sigh dropped her shoulders and her tummy relaxed. *Was* it fortunate that she'd recently divorced her soap opera star husband of twenty years who had been unfaithful for half that time? It had been a year and a half since Brock had left their home at her request. The divorce had been finalized a month ago. He had gotten more than he deserved. The house in Los Angeles, the Swiss vacation home. Their friends—Martha, her yoga buddy, was *such* a traitor! Pieces of her dignity.

Saralyn had to be out of the house by the end of summer. With no idea where she would land, she knew with certainty she did want to leave California and the bad memories it held. With a one-million-dollar settlement sitting in her bank account, she could begin again.

Beginning again was one of the reasons she now stood here in this quiet villa on a private Caribbean island. The other had to do with her career. A should-she-or-shouldn't-she? dilemma that must be resolved within the two-week stay.

Thanks to her friend Juliane's last-minute schedule change, Saralyn had the entire island to herself. Juliane had intended to stay here on a romantic getaway with her boyfriend. This island, after all, was where *Sex on The Beach* had been filmed. She'd been curious to check it out.

However, Juliane had gotten a call two days ago confirming she'd earned a seat on a six-month Antarctic research mission that was leaving immediately. An aquatic biologist, Juliane knew a refusal would bar the applicant from ever applying again. After accepting the position, she'd called Saralyn.

It hadn't taken more than a "you deserve this" and a "sunny skies and blue waters" from Juliane for Saralyn to accept the generous offer. The rental fee had been nonrefundable. And while the divorce settlement had been earmarked for her future home and retirement savings, she had received the final payment for the memoir she'd ghostwritten, so she could manage any expenses this trip presented.

Today was publication day for that memoir.

Sneering at her reflection, Saralyn silently admonished the foolish woman who had written the autobiography *Living Paradise*. The author's name on the cover? Brock Martin.

"Just let it go," she told the woman in the mirror. "He's out of your life. Start…a new chapter."

So here she was. Two weeks of blissful blue skies, turquoise waters, white sands and tropical weather. On *the* island. Yes, she had written the story that had been filmed here—she was contractually bound not to tell anyone, including Juliane, about that. And it thrilled her that she finally had opportunity to visit this place that she felt a proud connection to.

But during these two weeks she also intended to figure out her life. Where was she headed? Dare she allow love into her life again? How to even begin dating as a middle-aged introvert? And should she take the offer to ghostwrite another book for a *New York Times* bestselling romance author? Or did Saralyn dare to refuse that contract and instead write her own story, the historical-heist idea that had been nudging at her for years?

"You will figure it all out," she said to her reflection. "I know you can do it."

Nodding in agreement, but not completely feeling the assurance from her mirror self, she grabbed the bright, oversize pink silk scarf from the top of her suitcase and began to wrap it around her hips. Then she paused. Saralyn shook her head. No one here to see her cellulite or notice that her breasts weren't quite so high as they had been a decade earlier. And who needed makeup? She was unattached and alone and intended to embrace that refreshing freedom.

She tossed the scarf to the bed. It had only been a half hour since she'd set foot here. The guide who had driven the water taxi to the island had swiftly walked her through the villa placed but a stone's throw from the beach, pointing out the luxurious amenities—a fully stocked wine fridge!—and various spots of interests, but she'd known the layout. She'd watched the movie five times. The excitement of setting foot on this particular island could not be ignored.

Breezing through the living area, a vast half-circle room that featured curved windows three stories high—every view spectacular—she paused in the kitchen where a discreet black box sat under a cupboard. As she'd learned from the guide, it was a Faraday box. A person could place their electronic devices inside and it would block the island's Wi-Fi. No texts, no phone calls possible. Utter peace.

Clutching her phone to her chest, she eyed the box. While she wasn't a huge scroller, she did like to have it near for texts or calls from her mom. On the other hand, she had promised to check in with her, but only after she'd gotten settled.

"I'm going to do this vacation the right way."

She set the phone inside the box, then pulled her laptop from the carry bag, tucked it in, too, closed it and gave it a pat.

A wood walkway dotted with solar lights led her beneath a palm tree archway that sifted crisply in the light wind as she strolled toward the beach. Stepping onto the superfine, pearl-white sand, she delighted in the sensory warmth, wiggling her toes. Tilting back her head, she took in the azure sky, unreal in its utter blueness, and spread out her arms. The breeze tickled through her long brown hair, not pulled back in her requisite I'm-working ponytail. Her skin prickled as it awakened to the sunshine unadulterated by city smog. And the clear turquoise ocean glittered.

"Thank you, Juliane," she said.

Spying a set of wooden chaises, she wandered over—but before sitting, decided to wade into the water. Warmth splashed her ankles and her feet sank into the wet sand as she stepped in deeper. This felt too good to be real. During their twenty-year marriage, she and Brock had rarely vacationed. They'd used the Swiss getaway once, and he'd invited an obnoxious gang of friends along. Yet Saralyn had written many a story set in such gorgeous climes, with only the internet as her research. The real thing was…breathtaking. Surrounded by nature and no electronic devices to distract her. This was heaven! Only now, as her very being jittered anticipation and utter awe, did she understand how much she needed this escape. Tears ran down her cheeks.

"To a new and interesting chapter of my life," she said.

With a kick that splashed water and a dip to swirl her fingers across the surface, she waded back to shore and settled onto the chaise.

The island, owned by a young billionaire inventor, provided the ultimate luxury experience. Food was delivered every morning via a discreet drop-off box she'd seen when the landing boat had arrived. Juliane had selected the drop-off option as opposed to an on-site chef. Various sporty activities were available, including hiking trails, jet skiing, snorkeling, windsailing, and there was even a badminton court at the center of the island next to an infinity pool. Full Wi-Fi—apparently one could speak commands from anywhere and the AI would understand—a spa, yoga taught via Zoom. Everything was ultraluxe yet blended with the natural surroundings.

Digging her toes into the sand, she closed her eyes to the kiss of sunshine on her eyelids. Sea salt and earthy, verdant tones perfumed the air. "I could get used to this."

For a moment, she processed the sensory warmth, scents, sounds and eventually moved inward to notice her calm heartbeats. Not thundering as they so often did when she was forced to drive the 105 freeway. Over the years she'd become a literal recluse, only driving to places close to home. Saralyn had learned to be alone, even within her marriage.

And you're alone now. On a big island. With no means to leave. Who else knows about this island and could easily visit it while you're here?

Heartbeats picked up pace as her writer's brain

concocted anxiety-causing scenarios. What had she done? She'd just relegated herself to a private island, far from civilization—the mainland was a fifteen-minute boat ride—and if anyone did come here she would be like a sitting target. Alone. Unable to defend herself...

Shaking her head, Saralyn chased away the crazy thought. Her brain tended to think the worst, and her body reacted as if it were really happening. She pressed a palm over her chest to calm her rapid heartbeats.

"You're fine. You're a big girl. Nothing weird is going to happen. Just enjoy!"

Today, she'd relax and settle in, probably walk the island later to take it all in. She didn't intend to go schedule crazy. Though she did have a few items on her to-do list. First on the list?

"Figure out what I'm going to write next."

If she accepted the ghostwriting job for the romance novel, she'd receive a paycheck, which she did need to cover basic living expenses. And that was about all it covered.

The other option, if she chose *not* to ghostwrite, would be to finish the historical-heist idea and publish under her own name. That would be a roll of the dice. Could she even sell under her name? Saralyn had been a ghostwriter for two decades, her entire writing career. Writing for others had always suited her introverted self.

She enjoyed the journey of the story, handing it in, and walking away with a paycheck. No promoting, podcasts or anxiety-inducing book signings necessary. She rarely received credit for her writing; the author always put their name on the book. The nonfiction celebrity autobiographies she wrote did sometimes give her credit on the copyright page. But she'd never felt the need for that recognition.

Saralyn Martin had always been happiest standing in the background. Unnoticed. A literal ghost.

Until.

The divorce had changed her. She still hadn't figured it all out, but she did know one thing: she didn't want to be a ghost anymore. And that applied to all aspects of her life. But could she do it? Had she the gumption and courage to stand as her own woman and make a career for herself, support herself and, for the first time in her life, *not* rely on a man?

The contract she had been offered to ghostwrite was for another romance. The last story she'd written for the author, set on a tropical island, had been exceedingly successful. *Sex on the Beach* had been filmed on this very island. With no credit for Saralyn.

Yet there was the issue of being able to support herself. Ghostwriting paid well enough but never enough that she was able to save, to get ahead. Her entire writing career she'd been married to Brock and he had supported the two of them. Brock had encouraged her to continue with her writing. It was her creative outlet, a means to thrive. She hadn't been required to bring in a certain income.

There were times, though, she'd felt he may have squelched her desire to make more money, to try her hand at stepping beyond the ghostwriting and seeing how it would go under her own name. The earnings possibilities were far greater than ghostwriting.

Had Brock purposely kept her under his thumb, emotionally and financially? Keep the wife tucked away at home while he philandered? He'd never argued when she'd stepped back from attending a flashy event with him. The man had an ego. And she knew he couldn't abide being married to a woman who made more money than him, or who may have stolen the spotlight with a swing of her silken hair and a flash of her veneers. Or possibly, a woman who may have garnered her own fame through her bestselling novels.

Saralyn could craft a great story. And she had the skill to alter her on-the-page voice to match that of the authors she ghostwrote for. And in reviews, fans lauded the author's ability to craft the ultimate sexy hero. They dubbed him their "book boyfriend" and had even written sexy fan fiction about him.

Saralyn loved to read the reviews. And, yes, she did have a talent for creating a sexy alpha man on the page. Generally, he had dark hair and European features. Muscles for days. And he always knew when to walk around without a shirt on. He was aloof but attentive. Smart and fun. He always protected the heroine. And while he had his own goals, ambitions and dreams, he would walk the world and battle dragons to ensure the heroine was happy. The best men existed on the page.

Might she ever find another hero to walk into her life? Did they even exist in real life? Brock Martin had once been her hero. No longer. And really. Did she *need* a man to protect and care for her?

She shrugged. "I prefer my men on the page. Give me tall, dark and..."

She softened her focus and allowed the elements of an ultimate hero to coalesce before her. Tall, he walked proudly and perhaps with a slight bow to his legs. Something so sexy to her about a bowlegged walk. Arms swinging confidently with his strides, he mastered the earth with each step, the hero returning to claim all that he desired— which was only ever the heroine's heart.

His hair, dark as raven wings or coal dust or even precious black tourmaline would be carelessly finger-raked into a non-style, yet look as though a stylist had spent hours on it. Bedroom hair? Oh, yeah. A loose strand would probably dangle over his sharp but domineering eyebrow. Beneath those brows were eyes forged from earth and stone that caught the sunlight and told stories, so many tales of adventure, trial and heartbreak. The heroine could never look into those whiskey-brown irises without catching her breath and seeing her truth reflected back at her.

A chiseled jawline was de rigueur, along with the perfect amount of dark stubble. Not quite a beard, but never straggly. This man was perfection.

And farther down…

"Oh, yes, those abs." Saralyn blinked, loving the fantasy of bare torso and abs. They were hard. Honed. Tanned. The proverbial six-pack.

Licking her lips, her body softened, relaxing against the wood chaise as the sexy vision approached.

The man who walked across the beach toward her held a string of fish and wore his swim trunks low to reveal the cut muscles that looked hard enough to hone steel. Sweat pearled on those muscles—or no, those were water droplets from the ocean. A merman risen from the depths. Come to seduce her silly with a godlike physique and darkly devastating looks.

Saralyn tugged in her lower lip. The perfect amount of dark chest hair glinted with water droplets. Not too much that a woman would wake in the middle of the night dreaming of bears, and not so little that the sun would gleam on his bare skin. Masculinity defined. And he had...she counted... more than a six-pack. Mmm, wouldn't she like to wander her fingers over those hard ridges?

A brilliant glint sparkled between his lips as he curved a sun-shaming smile.

"Wait." Clutching the chaise arms, Saralyn sat upright. Was she hallucinating? She narrowed her gaze against the sunlight and then opened her eyes wide. The man was...real? Couldn't be.

"There's not supposed to be anyone on this island." Never had her imagination conjured the real thing.

Her heart stuttered. Had her worst fear come true? Alone on the island—he didn't look like a serial killer come to claim his next victim. But what a perfect ruse to lure the victim closer!

No. Chill, Saralyn. He's just one of the staff. A local? Or a fisherman who had anchored his boat nearby?

Whoever he was, he was stunning.

And she was a pale, middle-aged woman wearing a teeny bikini.

She stood, grasping for her silk scarf, then remembered she'd left it in the villa. Shoot! She clasped her hands across her tummy and nervously slid them upward. Then one hand slid to her hip where she sported that unasked-for menopausal bonus bulge.

"Who are you?" Body discomfort aside, this wasn't right. "This is *my* island."

"Is it, now?" A bemused smile glinted in the stranger's eyes. Dark irises, probably whiskey brown or even earthen umber. His mouth quirked in a seductive smirk, like a romance hero set to seduce the heroine with his charming aloofness. "Your island?"

"It is for the next two weeks," she said firmly. How dare he distract her annoyance with an inhale that flexed his pecs? "Are you staff? Is that my dinner?" She gestured toward the fish. "Is that what was meant by 'fresh food delivered daily'? That's taking things to the extreme."

With another flutter of her palm across her stomach, she sucked in. Did he notice her tummy? Her pale skin desperately in need of a tan? Why was the sexiest man alive standing so close to her she could feel her nipples harden and—that was so not what she needed right now.

"Dinner?" He jiggled the line of fish. "If you like. I'm willing to share."

Share? As in— Was he *staying* on the island?

"No seriously. Who are you?" she pleaded. "There must have been a booking mistake."

He offered a hand to shake, which she could but stare at. For as appealing as that hand looked, and it was attached to, oh, such a gorgeous physique, she did wonder if it was coated with fish slime. "I'm the owner of the island."

The...owner? That man was a billionaire who invented things and should—according to her writerly imagination—be wearing a lab coat or even a fancy business suit. Not looking like a sexy version of Robinson Crusoe.

"The owner," she said. "Sorry. I didn't know— but I did pay to stay here. Rather, I'm using my girlfriend's vacation since she had previous— Oh, it doesn't matter. This is *my* vacation. On a *private* island. *Private* meaning just me. No one else."

"That could be one definition of the word."

"There is only one definition of *private*," she protested.

"*Private* simply indicates the island is secluded. Set off from the rest of the busy world. I'll be here for a stay."

"But you... This is supposed to be a private island!"

"You keep saying that but the definition doesn't change. It *is* a private island."

The man showed no sign of understanding or complying with her desperate need to make him gone. "Not if there are two people on it!"

"I have a right to be here anytime I want. It's in the fine print."

"The fine print?" Saralyn had developed a need to wear readers for small text. It was not how she'd expected fifty to greet her. Why couldn't she age gracefully? But no matter. "I didn't read the contract."

"Not wise."

"As I've said, this vacation is my girlfriend's booking. She's the one who did all the paperwork and read…" Had Juliane read the fine print? What did it matter? The man should not be here!

Saralyn crossed her arms over her breasts. Who cared about her tummy bulge and cellulite? This was just wrong. How to relax and find her groove when Adonis wandered the island? And in nothing more than a pair of khaki swim trunks that seemed to fade from sight against his tan skin and enhance every single spectacular muscle on his body?

"No one ever reads the fine print," he offered with a shrug. "But don't worry. I won't get in your way. I use the island when I need it. And…" His heavy sigh gave her anxiety a pause. What did that world-weary sigh mean? "I really need it right now. I'll stay at the chef's cottage on the other side of the island. You won't see me. Unless you want to."

Unless she…? Had he said that with a lilting

tease? Cheeky of him. Yet it did prod an intriguing wedge into her plans. Alone on an island with a sexy stranger? Such a trope always appealed in romance novels.

"Well, I don't want to share," she forced herself to say to defeat her failing stoicism. "I want to enjoy this vacation as was intended, alone and…"

Alone and desperate? She wasn't desperate. Just…seeking. But she was thrown. Wasn't sure how to react with all that *man* and pulsing muscle and wet chest hair and gleaming teeth.

"I need to go change." She spun and headed to the villa.

"The bikini suits you!" he called.

Saralyn gestured dismissively behind her as she increased her speed. That he must see her thighs jiggle as she hurried off humiliated her. Once in the villa, she pulled the sliding-glass door shut and then the bamboo curtains. Only when she felt sure he could not see inside did she turn her back to the wall and blow out a breath.

A man who bore the physical appearance of every devastatingly handsome hero she'd ever created had just stepped off the page and barged into her reality. And he didn't seem at all concerned that she was bothered by it!

"This is not going to work."

CHAPTER TWO

THE WOMAN HE might have possibly frightened on the beach earlier was a knockout. Long legs, pale porcelain skin, soft brown hair. David couldn't help but notice how she had tried to cover her stomach, then her breasts. If women knew how most men's minds functioned—soft, pretty girl talking to me; score!—they wouldn't give their random body parts a second thought. Men did admire beauty, but it was the personal connection that really got their systems rolling.

At least, that's how it worked for David Crown. Good conversation and an attractive demeanor? Sign him up!

David had expected a couple to be staying on the island—he'd checked the schedule—and had intended to keep his distance while perhaps one day introducing himself and thanking them for their patronage. He'd not expected… He hadn't gotten her name. Who was that marvelous beauty possessed of a serious need to relax?

Whoever she was, she had just shoved a wrench

in his plan to work things out. The escape from reality part had been achieved. Owning this island served as the perfect getaway when the real world got too intense. Of course, his COO had his number and had called when he'd landed hours earlier. Reminding him that he could never completely escape The Dilemma. A decision needed to be made, and soon.

He'd carried a photo of a six-year-old boy in his wallet for weeks. His heart fractured even more every time he looked at the child's big bright eyes. That haunting smile was the reason he'd come here to make one of the biggest decisions in his life. It would happen before he returned to New York City.

But right now he was in curiosity mode. A much better place to occupy than grief. His escape from the real world had been disturbed by the presence of a lovely—yet annoyed—woman.

Of course, he was a man of his word. He'd not intrude on her privacy. Too much. Her face, free of makeup and absent those weird long false lashes most women wore, had gone from surprise to anger to worry after seeing him. He wanted to see it go to happiness.

So he knocked on the glass villa door. The curtains were drawn. He hoped not because of him. The best way to enjoy the island was with the two-story sliding-glass doors wide open to allow the tropics to intrude upon the harsh structure of shelter.

The curtain pulled aside to reveal big brown eyes and a straight mouth. Her hair was tidied into a queue at back and a soft white caftan hung off one bare shoulder. Inadvertently exquisite.

He lifted the plate of fish to show her why he'd come. He was no four-star chef, but he could fillet and grill a fish, thanks to lessons from the world-famous chef he employed.

With a reluctant nod, the woman slid open the door, but only five inches. She wasn't going to make this easy.

Fair enough. David often dealt with business execs and marketing pros who insisted their way was best. He had this.

"I come bearing the promised dinner and an apology."

One delicate dark brow arched on her face.

"My manner was rude and dismissive earlier. I apologize. We should have been properly introduced. And I shouldn't have assumed you would appreciate another person staying on *your* island."

Always let the other party feel they are in control.

She opened her mouth, but before she could speak, he added, "As well…" He splayed out his arms. He'd donned a crazy Hawaiian print shirt, which always made him smile at the wild colors, and a pair of beige cargo shorts. "You must have been utterly aghast to see a half-naked man stalking toward you on what should have been a *private* beach."

"Aghast?" She pressed a hand to her chest and then...chuckled. The dulcet sound zapped David's apprehensions and his shoulders dropped. "I do believe I was. Not so much because of all the abs and chest hair and—" She pressed her lips together and shook her head.

She had been studying his abs? David controlled the urge to smolder at her. He'd been told his smolder was irresistible. A panty-dropper, according to some silly social media site devoted to posting photos of him. So weird that people did that. Like stalking him, only it didn't make him feel threatened so much as creepily uncomfortable about all the comments regarding his physique and what the commenters would like to do with said physique.

"Let's leave it at *aghast*." She stepped aside and pushed the sliding door open; the ball bearings took it to rest on the opposite side of the room where the curve of the building began. "And dinner? I accept the apology." She held out her hand in wait of the plate.

David held it a little closer to his chest. He didn't intend to retreat too quickly. Not when he'd won the apology phase of this interesting scenario. "Might I come inside?"

She took an inordinate amount of time studying the plate and compressing her mouth. To let in the perfect stranger or to grab the food and slam the door in his face?

"I suppose."

Not the most promising invitation. "Well, if you're not sure?"

"You did cook. No reason we can't share a meal."

"Thank you." He stepped inside and set the plate on the kitchen counter, cut from a slab of pyrite-bespeckled lapis lazuli. He'd had the entire villa decorated with earthy tones and minerals and crystals from conflict-free mines. Turning, he offered his hand, which she had refused to shake earlier. "David Crown. Owner of the island, inventor, entrepreneur, philanthropist and genuinely apologetic."

She shook his hand, which was a good sign. "Saralyn Martin. Vacationer, writer and no longer aghast."

"Nice to meet you, Saralyn. The fish is cooling. Shall we share a meal and chat? I can fill you in on some of the island's more secret surprises. Then I promise to leave you to your isolation. It is what you paid for after all."

She went to the cupboard and retrieved plates,

glasses and a bottle of wine from the fridge and brought it to the table. "As I explained earlier, I didn't pay for it. My friend wasn't able to use the trip and she knew I needed a getaway. I never let opportunity pass me by. Or rather..." She considered what she'd said. "I won't anymore. All opportunities must be considered. Yes. I like that."

She set the plates on the table, across from one another, and then twisted the cork from the wine bottle. An easy twist. She'd already popped the cork? His admiration for the woman increased.

David moved one of the plates to the left so they could sit closer, and seated himself as she sat in her chair. He dished up the fish.

"That looks delicious and smells—" she inhaled, eyes closed as if smelling a flower "—like coconut?"

"I make the sauce using the coconuts on the island," he said. "All local ingredients."

"Are you a chef, too?"

He shrugged. "I like to experiment when I stay here. There are coconuts, fish, some berries and a generous variety of fruits, ripe for the picking this time of year. Though I suspect Ginger and Mary Ann might come up with something much more interesting."

Her eyebrow arched and her inquisitive brown eyes twinkled at his reference to the television show, *Gilligan's Island*, which had revolved around the lives of seven quirky castaways stranded for years on an island.

"I'm not so sure about their culinary adventures," she said. Their specialty was coconut cream pie. I always wonder about those two."

"How so?"

"Seriously? We all know the glamorous movie star, Ginger, never baked a day in her life. Sweet, wholesome Mary Ann, who once worked at a general store, did it all. Yet more often than not she let Ginger take the credit."

"Mary Ann was a people pleaser."

Saralyn exhaled and caught her elbows on the table, nodding. She'd drifted off somewhere and David felt sure it wasn't to an island populated by a professor, a millionaire and a movie star. One of his favorite old-timey shows to watch as a kid, he knew the characters well. "Do you know why the professor booked his tour on the *S.S. Minnow* that day?"

She gave it some thought. "I don't recall."

"He was doing research for his book *Fun with Ferns*," David provided. "I identify with the professor the most."

"Really? Oh, you did say you are an inventor. I guess I must claim Mary Ann's identity but with an ambition toward being the uninhibited and sexy Ginger." She trailed a finger along the plate before her and eyed him with interest.

"What's a young guy like you doing watching television shows from the sixties? Weren't kids of your generation into mutant turtles or Barney?"

"Barney. Ugh. That big purple puppet scared the daylight out of me. But you're not old enough to have watched the original series. Surely you watched the replays as I did?"

"If you're wrangling for my age you're going about it the wrong way."

"I wasn't." He nudged the plate toward her to distract from this conversational curve. One thing he did know about women was they could be touchy about their ages. "Try this?"

"Yes, of course." A few bites and some careful consideration. David watched an entire litany of sensory decisions glimmer in her eyes. Remarkable how outspoken she could be without saying a word. Finally, an approving nod. "I don't usually care for seafood but this is…just right. What kind of fish is this?"

He inwardly beamed at the compliment. She was either easy to impress or… Was she a people pleaser like Mary Ann?

"It's a kind of mackerel. I'm glad you like it because fish is it for my culinary skills."

"And this sauce is incredible. I give it four stars."

"I'll take it." He poured wine for them both.

"So, Professor, you mentioned earlier that you

had come here to escape." Over the rim of the glass, her intense brown eyes didn't so much prod as seek.

"Did I say that? Well, I did put that wording in the fine print so whenever I feel the real world crushing down on my shoulders I can retreat here."

"What's crushing you? What do you do, anyway? Besides own the most perfect tropical escape I've ever visited."

"Have you visited many?"

"Well." She touched her goblet, then shook her head. "But I have done research. And this is a fine example of private islands. The wine fridge alone has won me over."

"You do research?"

She ate another bite of fish and gestured with her fork. "No, we are on you right now. Your work and what's crushing your shoulders."

She got right to the point and was a careful foil to evasion. Smart woman. Not someone he suspected would easily accept a dismissive reply. Fair enough.

"I own Crown Corp. We invent 'remarkable things to change the ordinary world.'" He quoted the company motto. "I'm the chief scientist slash inventor. I'm also a philanthropist. Have a few charitable foundations. And I'm not known for my cooking."

"Then, no one has tasted your coconut fish."

"I save that culinary secret for my inner circle."

"That means I've already entered the circle." She sipped and gave him a steady stare over the goblet. "Nice."

His circle was small, but he wouldn't mind inviting her into it. And not simply as a friend to review his cooking skills. Those soft brown eyes pulled him in and he wasn't sure if he would drown or float in them. She wasn't openly flirting with him, but some undertone in her voice lured him deeper. Not like most women, he decided. At least, not the ones he'd dated.

"Crown Corp basically runs itself," he said. "I've some very trusted people running the show, but I like to keep my hands on the gears, so to speak. The lab is my usual hangout. I will never remove my inventor's apron and safety goggles. Ideas abound in my brain. Which means the concept of leisure is foreign to me. Usually takes me a day or two to unwind after I arrive here."

"Crown Corp? Is that…the hug blanket?"

"Yes, you know it?"

"Who doesn't? The commercial is on TV all the time. And…don't you donate blankets to children's hospitals and homeless shelters?"

"And women's shelters, and when there's a natural disaster, we ship directly to the relief site.

Helping others was the principal purpose for the blanket's invention."

"A blanket that actually hugs a person. That's crazy."

"You've never tried it?"

"No."

Surprising. It seemed his invention had literally blanketed the world, at least according to sales numbers. David was accustomed to friends, acquaintances, even the lady in the supermarket checkout—he liked to buy his own produce—regaling him of its beloved qualities.

And yet, the photo in his wallet reminded him that some things perhaps weren't meant to be shared with the world.

"I know we stock them in the villa." He scanned around the half-circle living area. "That blanket strewn artfully across the couch by the staging team is one of them."

She glanced to the cream-colored blanket which matched the interior's neutral wood, bamboo and sandy tones. "I'll give it a try later." She pushed her plate aside, having finished the fish, and propped an elbow on the table, her attention focused entirely on him.

Thankful she'd dismissed the blanket—he wasn't emotionally prepared to talk about it—he fell into her gaze. What a unique experience. For a woman to look at him like she was interested in what he had to say? Rarely did he talk shop with anyone. Most women he dated nodded absently while he could see their brains rushing to sensational queries like: *How rich are you? Do you really own a private jet? Can I get a photo for my socials? Did that princess really ban your blanket in her country because you wouldn't date her?* And the oft-asked question of late: *What about that trial, eh?*

"So, something with your business has got you seeking escape?" Saralyn prompted.

There it was. The question that stabbed at his too-tender heart. Did she *not* know? He'd thought the entire world aware of his struggles. Of that trial.

"Yes, something to do with the business." He quickly downed the rest of his wine and poured more.

"That question makes you uneasy." She tilted her head, studying him. And not in a surface manner, but rather, she seemed to permeate his very molecules and root about for atom-level truth. That both startled and intrigued him.

"I know we just met," she said, "but I'm interested in the deep delve. It's the writer in me who likes to step into a certain bold space."

"I can sense that."

"You do?" She bowed her head and smiled a little. Surprising herself with her boldness? What a lovely contradiction. "But also... I confess I have an intense desire to take control of my life. Be more assertive. So I'm going to ask the hard question. You can answer or not. What is *it* exactly?"

"Taking control of your life? Have you not had control over it?"

"Not me. You." She gestured with a finger toward him. "You're in the hot seat right now. What's the thing you're avoiding?"

Did she notice the sweat forming at his temples? He didn't like the interrogation, the morbid interest in a private matter. Fine. It was a Crown Corp matter. And mostly, the sensationalism of personal pain.

Yet Saralyn threatened in none of those ways.

He asked, "Promise you'll sit on the hot seat later?"

She considered the question, then nodded.

"Fine. Why am I here? It's to do with the lawsuit."

"A lawsuit? Against...you?"

"Do you not listen to the news?" he asked. "You've heard nothing about the legal travails of Crown Corp and its feckless CEO, David Crown?"

He did not like that label of *careless*. He was always concerned for the safety of others. Crown Corp could not have risen to such success had he not been adamant about safety.

"Sorry." She teased a fingertip around the rim of her wine goblet. "Another writer foible is that I tend to get lost on the page. Seclude myself from television and social media while working on a project. And with the past months…" She looked aside and shook her head. With an inhale, she lifted her head as if renewing her purpose. "I catch up on news now and then."

"Lost on the page." And what had happened in her past few months that she couldn't speak it? "You most certainly are getting on that hot seat later."

"Fair enough. So, a lawsuit?"

David pressed a thumb to his brow. It was much easier when a person knew the salacious details the media put out. Whether they were accurate details or not, at the very least they had a sketch.

"Crown Corp has been involved in a lawsuit…"

It was the reason he had escaped to the island. Not to talk it out, but rather to dive deep and discover the truth of his beliefs and determine if he could walk forward with the same integrity he'd always strived for.

If he didn't give her all the information, the self-proclaimed researcher could look it up and learn on her own.

"Legally, I can't give all the details." Mostly true. Though the trial was over and the transcripts had been released to the public. "Suffice, Crown Corp was cleared. It was an arduous two-week trial. I attended daily. And…" He caught his head against his hands and pushed his fingers through his hair. The tightness at his temples warned of an impending headache. He had to monitor his stress or it would flatten him like a steamroller. "I guess it messed with my head more than I thought it would. I've been snapping at employees lately. Not my style. Dodging the reporters that hang outside Crown Corp. The media has picked up on my distress, hyping me as heartless."

"Oh, my. I'm so sorry."

"I will never understand how the paparazzi seem to spring out from nowhere. No matter where a man goes, they are always there. Anyway, I needed to get away. Breathe this stunning fresh tropical air and get right with my heart."

She nodded. Understanding? "Well, I hope you find what you need while you're here. I can relate to getting right with one's heart."

"Yeah?" He could tell that they shared common struggles as he felt an enticing pull towards her. He saw a chance to turn the tables. "Your turn on the hot seat?"

"Fine. But I'm going to state this quickly, then jump off the seat. Because I'm still processing."

"Fair enough. Why your escape?"

"I got divorced about a year and a half ago. We were married twenty years."

David nodded. That would place her in her forties? Fifties?

"My ex was—rather *is*—a soap opera star. I stood on the edge of the Hollywood lifestyle the entire time, looking in, trying not to stumble on too much glitter. Anyway, I learned he had been screwing women on the side for ten of those years. The divorce was finalized last month. I walked away with enough to buy a house and start over. And he gets a ghostwritten memoir— today is the publication date—telling the world how fabulous he is. Thus, the need to take back my control. To rejoin life. And in the process, I've also to plot out a new book to satisfy my agent."

"Wow. That is some escape-the-world stuff. I'm sorry about the divorce."

"Don't be. It was meant to be. But it is tough to walk through the process of dissolving such a long attachment."

"I imagine so. And the book? I love a good novel."

"Really?" The light returned to her eyes, and that massaged the stab of regret David felt at asking about her escape. "Who is your favorite author?"

"The list is so long. Of course, I'm a King fan. He does average-Joe horror like no other. And

Koontz is a comfort read. I also enjoy a good action, heist story. And any mystery that doesn't involve a sweet little old lady knitting or baking cupcakes."

Saralyn's laughter was deep and refreshing. For a woman who sought to take back control, she owned the room with that confident laugh.

"Good call on the mysteries," she said. "I'm actually a ghostwriter. So you'll never see anything I've written on the bookshelves. Or actually, you'll see it, you just won't know I've written it. Another author's name is on the cover."

"No credit whatsoever?"

"Nope. And I don't mind. Or rather…"

She drifted to that thoughtful place again and he decided to let her go with it this time. Because his thoughtful place had become furnished with her soft hair and those telling brown eyes. Perfect bow lips and the smooth alabaster of her shoulders. Could he curl up and lose himself? An incessant desire for connection niggled at him. After so many failed relationships—or rather, they just hadn't been the right person for him— dare he hope for something real?

"I want to step up and be known," she declared. "The time has come to see *my* name on a book. To support myself. So my dilemma is… Should I ghostwrite another story for a well-known romance author? Or do I dare write the novel that's been prodding at me for years?"

"I vote for the novel that's prodding you. But what do I know? Do you need the ghostwriting gig to survive?"

"Yes and no. I'll be fine for a few years, but then I'll need to buckle down and support myself with my writing. And the thing is, can I do that as an unknown with my name on the cover? I'm not sure. Surely, it would pay more than the ghostwriting jobs, but selling is the issue."

"What does your agent say?"

"She thinks I would be a fool to let the ghostwriting gig slip from my fingers. It's a guaranteed paycheck, though I'm not sure I can support myself with it. I've always relied on my husband's income."

"Can you write both?"

"Not well. I'm a one-project-at-a-time writer. It's something I'm going to consider over the next two weeks. I want to leave this island with a sound plan for my future."

"I wish you luck."

"Thank you." She reached across the table, her hand nearing his, and then suddenly pulled back. Had she been about to take his hand? Offer a reassuring touch? His heart thundered to consider such. But she'd caught herself. Good call.

He didn't want to disappoint her. "I hope you find the peace you're seeking."

"This island never fails to calm me," he said. "I can loll in a hammock and read with waves sloshing in the background for hours."

"That's on my schedule for tomorrow. Along with a hike around the island to check out all it has to offer. I'm not sure I'm up for parasailing but kayaking and snorkeling could prove promising."

"If you intend to snorkel, you need to sign up on the portal so an instructor can come give you safety lessons and accompany you. It's all in the informational video."

She nodded toward the tablet computer set up on the kitchen counter, which provided twenty-four-hour support, information and guides for those guests who chose to do the completely staff-free experience. "Got it."

David felt the need to add, "I promise to stay out of your way."

"Oh? Uh… You don't need to do that. I owe you an apology, too. I was a bit harsh with you on the beach. Well, you did surprise me. Rendered me utterly aghast." Her smile was so delicious; it attacked her without warning, and he found that intriguing. "But there's no reason we must avoid each other, is there? I mean, I'm not inviting you to move in…"

"I get it. Maybe if you're lucky, I'll give you a spearfishing lesson one day."

"I might enjoy that. Sounds like good research."

"You're going to write a novel with a spear fisher in it?"

"I did that with the last novel I wrote for a romance author. It was set on a tropical island. Exactly like this one, in fact."

"And you're only now visiting one?"

"Yes, well, I'm a homebody. Not big on traveling where there are crowds or…" She sighed. "People. But that's going to change."

He could understand that fear of people, or rather, crowds, and when in lesser amounts, people he did not know. "I do need to point out one thing."

"What's that?"

"You said you want to rejoin life and to be known."

"I do."

"And yet, the place you come to prepare for that is a private island? Seems counterintuitive to me."

"Doesn't it?" Her laughter found a place in his core and spun gently. It wasn't a feeling he wanted to lose. "I'm starting slow. You know that Stella-getting-her-groove-back story?"

"Loved the movie."

"Well." She spread her arms out to her sides. "This is Saralyn *finding* her groove."

David lifted his goblet to toast. "To Saralyn finding her groove."

CHAPTER THREE

A HEAVY SIGH seeped from Saralyn's lungs as she tilted her head back against the beach chaise. It was early afternoon, and after a morning swim and a light lunch, she'd decided to laze awhile before hiking the island. Mentally, her gears were spinning. She didn't have to make the decision regarding her writing career in one day, but weighing her options was necessary.

If she accepted the ghostwriting offer, she'd have to write a ninety-thousand-word romance novel in five months. Hand it in. Cash the check. And be done. No edits because what she wrote then became the publisher's property. From that point, the author whose name went on the book cover in gold foiling—and who took all the credit for writing it on the copyright page—was allowed to do a light edit. From what Saralyn had read of the four published works she'd produced for that author, she hadn't changed more than an occasional name or car color. The gold-foil author earned royalties, got all the publicity and fame, and had even been the author of record when the publisher sold the last book to a movie producer.

Saralyn never complained about her ghostwriting gig. With each contract she got paid enough to live well for about half a year. And she had never been a spotlight seeker. Standing on the sidelines was her jam. The ghost no one had ever heard of or cared about.

Yet this island represented the achievement that she could not claim. The movie of her book had been filmed on this very sand. It was remarkable to be here. To take it all in. But it also reminded that she needed to step up, to grasp a new set of reins and finally take what she desired.

That being the other option, which was to not accept the ghostwriting contract. If she chose not to, her agent, Leslie, had warned she might never get another offer from that publisher. And Leslie had implied that if she was so stupid as to not take the offer, she wouldn't continue representing her.

Tough words to hear after a fifteen-year relationship with the agency. But Leslie had become complacent. She no longer sought writing jobs for Saralyn, she simply sat back and waited for the offers to come to her through publishers who had previously contracted with Saralyn. That oddball idea for the history of the bath that Saralyn had pitched her two years ago? Her agent had sniffed and said she didn't think her present stable of publishers would be interested. Well, certainly they may not be, but weren't there plenty other publishers out there? Why not shop it around? That, and the fact Leslie rarely negotiated for film royalties bothered Saralyn. Yes, her work was take the paycheck, no royalties, move on. But shouldn't she be compensated if it sold for film or screen?

Anyway, not accepting the ghostwriting job would allow her to work on the story she'd been chasing in her dreams for years. The historical heist with a twist. Set in eighteenth-century Paris, her favorite time period and location. She'd already drafted a third of the story. Had written detailed studies for the characters. And she'd worked out the impossible timeline. The twist was killer! The interesting characters beckoned to her. She just needed some time and space to focus and write it.

But writing a novel on spec would bring in exactly zero dollars to her coffers. And while Saralyn had the divorce settlement, she would rely on her writing to pay for groceries and basic living expenses. She would also need a car since Brock had managed to retain all three vehicles in the settlement. Truthfully, she'd easily given up on trying to keep any of their shared possessions. She'd simply wanted out and to remove as much of his unfaithful DNA from her life. Walking away with cash and no shared marital possessions had felt empowering. And it still did.

The future was hers to design. Yet what to do? To continue to ghostwrite or dare to write under her own name?

And what was that delicious scent that fluttered around her like invisible butterflies? She leaned to the side, slapping a palm onto the warm sand and tilted her head to study the trees and foliage behind her that edged the beach. Must be a tropical flower in there somewhere. The urge to bring along her phone so she could look up the flora and fauna had been strong, but...

"Maybe a few days before I leave," she decided. "I do have to take advantage of this hands-on research while I've the chance."

When she'd written the tropical island romance, she had wanted to visit an island to experience the sights, sounds and scents. Honestly, a writer need never leave their chairs for all the sensory details one could find online regarding any thing, place, emotion, etcetera. But she'd begun researching Brock's memoir at the same time. And that had made her physically ill. Escaping to a tropical island couldn't have happened with a queasy gut and broken heart.

Saralyn had discovered more than she'd wanted

to learn while researching Brock. As soon as she'd handed in the romance, she'd called a lawyer. At the time, she'd wanted to be discreet. Saralyn Martin was a ghost who was accustomed to standing in the shadows, accepting whatever role she was required to play in her famous husband's life, as long as she was treated well and kindly. She'd always felt that Brock cared about her. Even the last eight or so years when his attention had noticeably waned.

Had it been her fault his attention had wandered? Of course it had. She blamed herself for being so busy with her writing, not paying him enough attention. Call it an introvert's fear of parties or call it not feeling up to shining as brightly as was required of a Hollywood star's spouse. Once she'd had domestic dreams of family, children and the proverbial white picket fence. Saralyn had never fallen into the groove of the rich and famous. After only a few years of their marriage, Brock had stopped asking her to attend functions with him.

Truly, she had written herself into her own disastrous marriage.

Now? She wished she had blasted her research on all the news stations and social media. Let them know Brock Martin was an asshole who had cheated on her for half their marriage. A man who had insisted his wife remain in the background, write in the shadows, never stepping up and into the spotlight. But instead, meek and ghosty Saralyn had wanted to ensure no feathers were ruffled, that she wasn't drawn into the media frenzy, and had quietly settled. And at her agent's nudging, she'd even honored the stipulation that she finish writing her husband's autobiography because she was contractually bound. Leslie lost more points for not standing in her corner on that one.

Brock's memoir, *Living Paradise*, had been released yesterday. With his name in gold foil on the cover and no acknowledgement on the copyright page that Saralyn had written it all. It was a glowing narrative of his two decades on the soap opera scene. No mention about his hidden fixation with hooking up with young Botoxed blondes who he tended to promise a sit-down with his agent. Never happened. But Brock had gotten a few nights of sex out of those nubile ingenues. All of it, Saralyn had learned from going through his texts and emails. Tech-savvy and unbreakable passwords were not Brock Martin's forte.

"You are such a pushover," she muttered. Feeling the heavy weight of her past decisions, she slipped off the chaise and onto the sand, rolling to her back and stretching out her arms. "Can you really stop being a ghost? Do you dare?"

Next week, she turned fifty. Half her life gone.

And what had she to show for it? A few rare acknowledgements on some copyright pages and a failed marriage. Not to mention the menopausal pudge that she certainly hoped David hadn't taken note of.

The second half of her life had to improve. It could only get better, right? What she'd said to David in a moment of self-confidence about finding her groove had been exactly right. Saralyn Martin—make that Saralyn Hayes, her maiden name—needed to take back—no, to *create*—her life.

Might finding her groove include an affair with a younger man?

Saralyn spit out the few sand granules that dusted her lips. She was thinking like some kind of romance heroine if she thought the billionaire inventor would have an interest in her.

Though, the way he did look at her...as if she were the only person in the room.

"You *are* the only one in the room and on the island," she chastised her hopeful thoughts. "And he's too young. You don't want to humiliate yourself anymore by engaging in silly fantasies. Just stick to the plot."

A boring, cliché plot. That definitely needed some tweaking.

David spied the woman lying arms outstretched on the sand beside the chaise. Had she passed out? Been attacked by one of the aggressive island parrots that tended to fly low to a person's head if they were eating? Washed ashore after a vigorous swim had resulted in a poisonous jellyfish sting? There were no jellyfish, but his imagination could not be corralled.

She wasn't moving.

Thinking the worst, he rushed to her side. "Saralyn?"

"Oh, my God, there you are, like some kind of—" she sat up, brushed sand from her thighs and shook her head "—rescuing hero."

"Sorry. Not for rescuing you. You didn't need— It's not every day I find a woman lying sprawled on the sand as if she'd been attacked by wild parrots or a man-eating jellyfish."

"Man-eating— Are there jellyfish in the water?"

"There are not. It's just my inventor's brain. Sometimes it takes an imaginative leap and my body reacts as if it's really happening. Adrenaline."

"Been there, done that. Writer's brains can be the same. I can reduce myself to tears thinking terrible thoughts. But don't worry. I was…"

"It's okay. You don't need to explain. I'm not supposed to be bothering you." He stood yet didn't feel the urge to leave her because…beautiful and interesting woman. And he had her all to himself. Yet he sensed a deep sadness in her posture of dropped shoulders and bowed head. And she had been sprawled in the sand as if a water-starved starfish. "*Is* everything okay?"

That he'd asked surprised him. He did worry after others, but he rarely knew how to voice that concern. Showing empathy was something that made him feel extremely uncomfortable. Did he do it right? Or make it worse? Would it be offensive to offer a gentle touch or handhold? He just didn't know what was proper.

"I'm working on it." She brushed sand from her long, smooth legs. A slide of her palm across her stomach resulted in her sucking it in. "Just trying to figure out the rest of my life."

"Is that all?" He squatted beside her, making sure to keep a few feet of space between them. He didn't want her to feel as though he were imposing on her privacy. "How's that working for you?"

She opened her mouth to reply but her eyes suddenly diverted to what he held. "Do you always walk around with a machete in hand?"

He remembered the blade and sheepishly waved it before him. "I'm collecting coconuts."

"That's a better explanation than plotting my murder."

"No need for that. Your bill is already paid. And I don't have the first clue on how to hide a body."

"Good to know. So, coconuts? I've seen them up in the trees. They are all green."

"Best time to harvest them. They are sweeter when they are young."

"Young and sweet," she said, savoring the words on her tongue.

Was that a hungry look she gave him? And her voice had taken on a deeper, sexy tone.

"Oh." She shook her head and seemed to come back from wherever she'd drifted. "Don't mind me. I slip into plot mode at the worst of times."

"It's because I'm a terrible conversationalist, isn't it?"

"Oh, darling, we haven't had a real conversation yet. Oh, for a soul-deep conversation," she pleaded to what he could only imagine was the universe.

He felt much the same. When was the last time a woman sat down and talked to him? And really listened? They had shared their reasons for fleeing to the island last night. That had lifted something from his shoulders that he couldn't quite name but felt relieved for having shared.

"I'd like to have a conversation with you," he said. "But I'm aware that I am infringing on your privacy so—"

"Infringe away. I need a break from life planning. Will you show me how you harvest coconuts?"

"I'd love to."

* * *

A while later, Saralyn sipped sweet coconut milk from one half of the green fruit David had opened with an expert slash of the machete. He'd shimmied up the gracefully curved palm, like a monkey, and half a dozen coconuts had dropped to the sand after he'd called out, "Fore!"

She'd laughed at the golf reference. He'd explained he hadn't any other way to warn of impending flying spheres.

"What is that beautiful bird song?" she asked as she pried at the coconut meat with a fingertip.

"Some sort of tanager. They are tiny and bright scarlet. A portion of their wings flash emerald. They keep out of sight but enjoy serenading the island inhabitants."

"I could listen to them sing all day."

"A spoon works best." He gestured to her efforts. He'd collected half a dozen coconuts and put them in a woven bag. Wielding the machete, it caught the sun and glinted. "Do you want to try your hand at cutting one open?"

"I think I'll pass. I need all my fingers to type. Thanks for teaching me Coconut Harvesting 101. I'll definitely use it in a story someday."

He plopped down on the sand before her, squatting with his feet planted and his knees by his chest. Again he wore just the swim trunks. It was perhaps his island costume. With the temperate weather, it made sense. And it suited him more than she imagined a business suit might. If this man were to walk into her home office and flash his charming smile at her she would never get any work done.

"Did you know coconuts are considered a fruit, a nut *and* a seed?" he asked.

"I have come across that in my research but had forgotten about it. I take in information, use it, then it gets lost. But…something about it not being an actual tree seems to ring a bell?"

"Right. The coconut palm doesn't have bark or branches so it's not an official tree. I forget what the name is for the perennial. I'm like you. I take in a lot of info, keep the stuff that is meaningful and let the rest go. Though, don't you think it's all in there somewhere? Waiting to be retrieved?"

"Possible." She munched a piece of coconut meat. "If all the research and characters I've used over the years were always fore in my brain I'd go mad. There has to be a vault somewhere in our brains for storing the stuff that is no longer needed."

"So as a ghostwriter does that mean no one ever knows that you're the person who wrote it?" he asked.

"Exactly. I'm contractually bound to never reveal I'm the author. Though in a few cases I am given an acknowledgement on the copyright page. That's more like work-for-hire stuff. I've also written for an ongoing series that includes more than one author. We all wrote under one made-up author name placed on the cover. It was an adventure series featuring a female archaeologist who wielded Joan of Arc's magical sword. She could take out bad guys with a slash of her sword. It was a kick."

"It's remarkable that you've such restraint. I don't know if I could keep a secret like that. And forever?"

She laughed. "It's easy enough. I like to take the money and run. Though, I've had a change of heart after…well…" She shrugged. "The divorce."

"Twenty years is a long time. You should be proud of the accomplishment."

"Yes, I'm an old lady. Been around the track a time or two. And have the baggage to prove it. And I've taken my punches. Now I'm trying to get back up on the proverbial horse and—I've run out of clichés. On another note, I'm celebrating my fiftieth birthday next week."

"I never would have guessed."

"You don't need to be kind."

"Fifty isn't old."

"I've never thought it was. Until I learned that my husband had been screwing women half my age."

"That's rough. I'm glad you had the courage

to walk away from him. No woman should be treated as an afterthought."

She smirked. "I feel as though I brought it upon myself. There's a certain amount of guilt that comes from knowing I didn't try hard enough. An afterthought is exactly what I've accepted in my love life and my career. The woman no one pays any mind to. The one who does all the work and gets none of the credit. But enough moaning." Had she really spilled all that to him? Saralyn! Divert the point of view. Now. "How old are you?"

"Thirty-five."

"So your parents must be in their…fifties?" Mercy, they were closer to her age than he was.

Saralyn, what the hell? Drop all fantasies of an affair with a younger man right now!

"Mum is sixty, Dad a few years older."

Wasn't like she was considering doing anything with him anyway. Fantasies were fantasies for a reason. Because they couldn't, and shouldn't, become reality. She must stick to merely studying him as romance-hero material. Although, every time he stood near, her entire body seemed to reach for him. Desired a new plaything. And that she was even thinking of him as a plaything startled her. She was not that woman.

Was she? No.

Maybe.

He leaned closer and bent to catch her gaze. "I don't know where your thought process is taking you, but I will toss out the fact that age means nothing to me. I know people from your generation tend to look askance at couples separated by large age gaps. But really, my generation doesn't like to label or assign expected conditions."

"'Your generation'? 'Askance'? Oh, brother."

He chuckled. "Don't think about it too much, Saralyn. You are a beautiful woman. You intrigue me. I like a smart woman."

"Is that so?"

He nodded. "It's hard to find someone I can talk to."

"Maybe you're looking in the wrong places? I mean, there are literally billions of women out there. Of all ages."

"There are. And yet…" Standing, he snatched up the bag of coconuts and claimed the machete. "The crazy thing is the one who intrigues me most feels unattainable."

He swung the bag over a shoulder. "You know, you can take the meat out of that coconut and use it to cook. Maybe even—" he winked and it was such a cocky, charming move Saralyn felt it enter her heart like an arrow shot true "—make a coconut cream pie."

With that he wandered off, leaving her clutching the coconut to her chest as she watched his exit. His legs had a slight bow to them. His stride was confident and sure. The muscles across his back advertised an undulating landscape no woman could resist exploring. So alluring. A dashing specimen of man.

"So. Much. Man."

She thought about what he'd said. Was *she* the one who intrigued him? Words to make any woman's heart flutter. And swoon.

She didn't swoon. That was silly girl stuff. She was a grown woman who had been married, had gone through a devastating divorce and knew what it was she wanted and didn't want from a partner. She didn't want a creep who thought he could gaslight her and have women on the side. Nor did she want an inexperienced young pup who wasn't ready to settle. She did want…

What *did* she want in a man? Because she did crave a relationship. The divorce had not destroyed the part of her that enjoyed being a couple, having conversations and sharing life. She'd not gotten that from Brock. The craving had always been there, and it remained in an inaccessible chamber of her heart.

But she wasn't going to jump into happily-ever-after with a man she'd only just met. A man who knew one of her favorite television shows as well as she did. Sweet, people-pleasing Mary Ann had always had a thing for the handsome, smart professor…

She studied the coconut's innards, thinking if she were to scrape out the meat it would make a rather tiny pie. And how to make a crust? She'd never been much for baking. Frozen chocolate chip cookies popped in the oven were about her speed.

Would it please David if she did make a pie for him? Just like…

She tossed the coconut aside with a thrust. "What are you doing? You were going to stop being such a Mary Ann!"

The man had wriggled under her skin with his charming words and bedroom eyes. He'd even intimated that they might be… Well, he had only stated that age didn't mean a thing to him. He'd not implied they could have a thing. An affair. A tropical island tryst.

So why was she thinking about all those things and more?

CHAPTER FOUR

DAY THREE DELIVERED more island luxury. Following a swim, Saralyn lounged on the chaise, sunning herself. The sunshine here was ineffable. It was warm but not hot. Bright but not searing. Her pale skin did not burn and was tanning nicely. It was like someone had manufactured the perfect sun and hung it directly above her. Add in the barest of breezes that wafted the gorgeous scent of tropical flowers about her like perfume, and she was in heaven.

Yet the day could get more perfect. Currently, a half-clad hero wandered across the sand, having swam up from Atlantis. He smiled at her and waved a little.

Saralyn lifted her chin in acknowledgment. Couldn't appear too desperate for conversation. Though, in truth, she craved it more than she thought she should. Her life and job had been comprised of solitude. Save the weekly phone call to her mom. Divorce showed a person who their real friends were. Ninety-nine percent of them had sided with Brock and she hadn't heard from them since. That Martha from yoga had hoped Saralyn could introduce her to Brock's agent had only come out that last session at the yoga studio when Martha had told her she couldn't speak to her now that she'd dumped Brock. Juliane was her one bright light, and now she would be physically incommunicado for the next six months. The intrepid biologist had promised to FaceTime as soon as she got settled in her new chilly digs.

"Do you mind if I join you?" David asked as he approached the empty chaise but two feet from her.

"It's your island," she said dismissively.

Best to keep the fantasy just that, she told herself.

Don't fall into the story of a wild and crazy affair with the handsome young man. Heartbreak hurts.

With a tug to her wide-brimmed straw hat to shade her eyes, she tilted her head against the chaise.

"If that's not an encouraging invitation, I don't know what is." He settled next to her, his motion sweeping sand over her toes.

She wiggled those toes. Her body stirred at his closeness, once again vying to reach for him in an immaterial yet intense way. It had been a while since she'd sat alone with a man. It was never the same as sitting alongside a girlfriend. Men smelled better than perfume and cosmetics. They exuded a sense of presence, of being, that always intrigued her. A certain intimacy sparked. And it was never simple.

"I won't talk," he said. "One thing I do know about you is that you like your privacy. I just want to sit here and let the sun dry me off from the swim."

"Suit yourself."

And so began the most maddening ten minutes of her entire life.

Saralyn was not about to turn her head to see if he looked at her. Couldn't risk him flashing her that charismatic smile, knowing he'd made her look. Nor would she pull up her legs and wrap her arms around her knees to cover her stomach. She lay stretched out, arms hanging loosely and fingers digging into the sand at her sides. Any movement would surely call attention to the cellulite that jiggled on her thighs. And—she did subtly suck in her gut.

No!

Her conscience screamed so loudly she almost cast a glance to the side to make sure he hadn't heard.

Just relax. Be...normal. As normal as an introverted word-slinger can be. The man doesn't care what you look like.

Or he shouldn't. She was not on this island to have an affair with the sexiest, most gorgeous, best-smelling human she had seen, heard or inhaled in...

Ever.

Saralyn closed her eyes and sank into the presence of him. He smelled like the ocean, salty and crystalline. Yet a deeper undernote of rugged masculinity rose to curl across her skin, tickle into her senses, and tighten her nipples.

Shoot. Her bikini top was a wild riot of bright tropical flowers set against a deep green background. Difficult for anyone to see what was going on under the fabric. She hoped.

Chill, Saralyn. The more you react, the more he'll notice. Just...smell him. Savor him. Enjoy the temptation like you've never allowed yourself before.

Because she'd never been so tempted by a man.

One truth she had accepted following the divorce was that she'd lost herself in her marriage. After she'd stopped attending parties and screening events with Brock, she'd become very much a hermit. Life had revolved around research and writing. Only the occasional morning jog around the neighborhood to get her creative brain churning. Yet there had been that one neighbor... Sexy, tall, blond hair and blue eyes. He'd always smile at her and wave. Yet she'd never allowed herself to think about him when alone, to imagine, to fantasize. She had literally castrated herself from enjoying the sight of other men. Which wasn't right. Even in healthy, monogamous relationships, the couple looked at others. It was human nature.

But she'd wanted to be the good wife. The one Brock was never ashamed to be seen with, or to talk about. The housewife who sent him off in the mornings with a mug of coffee and a kiss and who had a meal waiting for him when he arrived home at night. Yet it had quickly become a function performed by rote. The morning kiss. The late-night meal that she'd sit and watch him eat because she had eaten hours earlier at the normal dinnertime. They'd share a brief conversation about his day at work. She'd tell him how many pages she'd written. The mention of an event might come up. Brock would always leave her an out. "It's not really for spouses, you can stay home." Or, "Me and a couple of the guys from work are having a few drinks." And she would nod and apologize for nothing she had done, and he'd wink and say she was a good wife.

A good wife who hadn't been attentive enough.

A good wife who had been oblivious to her husband's affairs.

Had he even attended some of those spouse-less events? Through a bit of detective work, she had learned he had not. Brock had kept an apartment by the beach and had used it often. The emotional carnage resulting from that research had knocked her flat in bed for weeks. Going through with the divorce had further stripped her of any dignity and self-love she possessed.

Running to her mother's arms back in Iowa had felt as if she was giving up everything, so she'd forced herself to stay in her and Brock's home and insisted he vacate. At the very least, she'd maintained her ground. Until the settlement had ruled in Brock's favor to keep the home he had initially owned before they'd met. Fair enough. She would never completely surface from the humiliation of her failed marriage while still occupying the very place where it had all happened.

It was sad to realize how much she had lost in her marriage. And when a tear jiggled at the corner of her eye, she quickly swiped it away and sat up. Enough of this feeling sorry for herself. She'd done that.

"Well," she stated. "You're rather quiet today."

David shifted on the chaise, bending up one leg. The sex appeal conferred in that one dark-haired leg was off the scale. "I didn't want to disturb you."

"I appreciate your discretion. But I'm a big girl. If I need privacy I can find it for myself."

"So you can. I have to say, though…" He turned and propped an elbow on the chaise arm, leaning his head against the back. He'd developed a five o'clock shadow that only enhanced his sexy appeal. "Sitting here alongside you and *not* talking? That was kind of cool. I mean, I've never simply shared the air with a person like this before. I closed my eyes and focused on the sounds of the waves and the birds."

Birds? There had been birds? Saralyn's focus had been entirely different, but well, people were weird like that. One person's point of view was never going to be the same as the one sitting next to them. Especially if the other person had rock-hard abs.

"Thank you," he said.

She shrugged. If he were privy to her thoughts, he may not be so appreciative. She hadn't moved to any sex fantasies. The man was safe from those shameless mind forays. For now.

Ah, heck, she didn't have to play the uptight matron. As well, she couldn't sit on the beach every day and pout over a big life decision. Time to start carving out her groove.

"So, tell me what a girl has to do to find a little fun on this island?" she announced. "I did check out the swings by the dock. I remember swinging so high when I was a kid and then jumping to land in the nearby sandbox."

"You can do the same with the swings here but you land in the ocean."

"I know. I did it." The confession tickled at her confidence. It had been a fun jump and in that moment she truly had felt like a kid again.

"There are kayaks in the storage shed."

That sounded like a fun challenge to the old dog who desperately needed to learn some new tricks. "I've never tried kayaking."

"It's pretty basic. I can teach you."

"Kayaks look like they might easily topple."

"They don't. And if they do, you know how to swim. Shall I go grab the kayaks?"

Spend an afternoon kayaking with a man whose every movement drew her attention as if some kind of rare being? A little adventure never hurt anyone. And she needed that balance between what could become two weeks of sulking, muddling over her failure of a life, and what to do next.

Time to start living her life.

"Let's do it."

When Saralyn decided to let go of whatever anxieties life had heaped on her, she shone.

It didn't take long for her to catch on to the balance and rowing skills, and soon they had kayaked the three-kilometer circumference of the island. The waters on the villa side of the island were so clear and icy blue they allowed one to marvel over the fish swimming beneath them. Sight of the swings had sparked Saralyn's soul-enlivening laughter as she sped ahead of him. The seats hung six to twelve inches above water, depending on the tides.

David hadn't paddled nearly as fast as he could. He had no desire to win this race because the prize for second place was a happy woman whose big brown eyes danced as she sought his approval. No, it wasn't necessarily approval; perhaps she was only looking to see if he shared her joy. He most definitely did. If he had landed on the island when it hadn't been booked, he would have been alone, and likely would have moped for days. This woman encouraged him to avoid that fruitless muddle. And he was thankful for that.

Reaching the swings, she shouted in triumph and pumped the air with a fist. He floated next to her and held her kayak securely as she got out to claim a swing. Hooking their kayaks to one of the big poles that supported the swing frame, he joined her on the other one.

"That was fun," she announced as she pumped her legs and splashed her feet across the water's surface.

More than she could know. Elation lightened his being. Surely it had been months since he had smiled.

Oh, that poor boy's smile. He had only lived six years... Don't think about that now!

With a nod, David pushed down the depressive thought. He'd initially expected to be consigned to the chef's cottage, but Saralyn was blossoming and opening up in a surprising manner, which in turn prompted him to do the same.

"This place makes me feel like a kid." She settled her swing to a modest sway beside him. "I want to kayak every day."

"Any day. Any time," he offered. "I'll keep them anchored here so they're available whenever you feel the urge."

"I think it's my charming teacher that made it so fun." She tilted her head aside the rope that suspended her swing seat. "Thanks for taking the time to show me how to kayak."

"I've got all the time in the world. No business meetings. Nothing to distract me. Save you. You know you're beautiful when you laugh."

She made a humming noise, considering it, then shrugged. "Thanks. I even forgot that I was wearing a skimpy bikini and dove into the experience."

"What's wrong with your bikini? I love the wild riot of colors."

"Sure, it is pretty, but...well. You must know how we women are about our bodies."

"I don't understand why women are so self-conscious about their bodies. I mean, you're all beautiful in your own way. What I like the most is the uniqueness of us all. There's not one person who is the same as the other."

"Twins."

"I'll give you that. You do know it's not so much the package you're in as your personality and smarts that attracts most men?"

"Tell that to all of Hollywood. I've spent the last two decades in Los Angeles. The home of the nipped, tucked, plumped and Botoxed. It's a mindset."

"A terrible one."

She sighed heavily. This was not the way he wanted the conversation to go. She'd been so elated.

"Do the women you write about put themselves down about their looks?" he asked.

"Not always. I write smart, focused women. Women who don't need a man but learn that it's nice to have a man around."

"Yikes. As an accessory?"

"Not like that. I mean… I tend to incorporate some of *my* beliefs when creating a strong heroine. Smart women who may not need a man, but like having them in their lives. Men are good for the female heart. And useful. Some of us aren't afraid to admit we like it when a man cares for us."

"Are you one of those 'us'?"

"I am. And I'm not so put off on the entire species of men just because my marriage failed. I'm open to whatever comes next for me."

"That's encouraging, but I'm a little stuck on the word *useful*. Like how? Fixing things? Changing the lightbulbs? Painting the house? Slaying the dragons?"

"Exactly!"

Again, her laughter bubbled out and David found himself reaching for her hand. She didn't notice, still clutching the swing rope, so he let his hand drop into the water. So close to contact with her warm, effervescent…beingness. He surprised himself he'd even made such a move. Hand-holding always felt like a task. Like a *function* he should perform and not a natural motion.

Her laugh stopped abruptly. "What? Did I say something wrong?"

"Not at all. I like listening to you laugh."

"Well." Regaining some composure, she sat up straighter and kicked her legs to sway the swing. "That's just weird."

"Then, call me weird. I don't think I would have succeeded with Crown Corp if I didn't toe the weird line."

"Probably not. You're an inventor so you have to be creative. We weirdos are the creative ones. The ones who dream big."

"What's your biggest dream?"

"Hmm."

As she considered the question, he considered her. Turning fifty? She didn't look a day over, well, he wasn't good with ages, but he'd place her at a solid late thirties, early forties. Her skin was smooth with only the faintest of creases at the corners of her eyes. Her body was shapely and toned, and—what parts of her did she not like? He couldn't stop wondering what it would be like to touch her skin. To bury his nose in her hair. To lean in and kiss her.

Yes, he wanted to kiss her. Not because he was alone with her on an island and it seemed the thing to do, but because she had drawn him into her aura and it felt sticky in the best way. He didn't want to disentangle himself from the energy she put out. It called to him. Lured him…

"After I leave the island, I'd like to walk into a new life," she said.

David sat up straighter, realizing he'd leaned so close to her that the swing had wobbled. Caught in a dream? It had been a good one.

A new life? "And what does that life look like?"

"A new place to live. In a different state. Maybe Arizona or even Maine. I'm not sure yet. I'm from Iowa. Lived there until my early twenties."

"That place gets as cold as New York. As does Maine."

"Yes, and while I love the snow, I've become accustomed to sun and warmth. I don't foresee shoveling in my future."

"Sounds wise. And in your new life, will you still be writing?"

"Yes, but will I be writing for myself or as a ghost?"

"Right. What does your dream say about that?"

"My dream says I'll be writing under my own name, getting paid well, and having readers actually know who I am. Fame? I crave that recognition."

That was interesting. And it was the first flaw he'd seen in her. "Fame doesn't come in bits. It's usually big and bold and in-your-face."

"I'll take it."

David tilted his head. "That surprises me."

"As someone used to being alone all the time, it also surprises me. But I'm all about not being a ghost anymore. People need to know who Saralyn Martin is. Or rather, Saralyn Hayes. I'm going to take back my maiden name. It feels strange to keep using my ex's surname."

"I hope you get what you desire. So you've made the decision to write that story under your name instead of the ghostwritten one?"

"Well."

That she didn't expound meant her dream may remain a dream. He sensed that she needed to jump beyond the closeted, quiet life she had led so far. However, from what he knew about fame, he didn't wish that for her. Not for anyone.

"I suppose you've already achieved your dream, eh?" she asked.

"The company? Yes, Crown Corp's success is a dream."

"'Remarkable things to change the ordinary world,'" she recited the motto he'd told her. "I love that."

"Yes, but I never set out to make billions."

"You just wanted to help others with a blanket that would hug them. I haven't tried the blanket yet. It's so warm there's no need for it."

"Sometimes a person just needs a hug," he said. "It's always there for that."

"You must be a master hugger if that was your raison d'être for creating the blanket."

"Me?" The idea of a hug made him…yearn. "Nah. I've never…"

A nervous tickle crept up David's spine. It was never easy to explain he'd created the blanket because he hadn't been given hugs as a child. Had always desired one. So when he was finally capable he'd created his own hug. It was similar to holding hands. Hugs and handholds felt foreign to him. Unattainable. And yet, it was all that he desired. The comfort with another person to really let go and accept what he'd never been given.

Yet that manufactured hug had been sullied by the trial. Truly, could he continue to produce the blanket and still maintain his integrity?

"I'm hungry," he said. Distraction was his only move when it came to avoiding his truths. "Do you want to come over to my place for some dinner?"

Saralyn's mind-reading gaze scanned his face a few seconds before nodding. "Sure, but you know I've got those chef meals delivered daily. And they feed two. Why don't you come over to my place?"

"It's a date."

"Oh, it's…" She stood from the swing, the water level midthigh. With a lift of her shoulders she said, "Yes, a date. Just us. The two of us— I'm going to run ahead and take a shower and change. Give me an hour to get a meal ready?"

"Of course."

She wandered to the beach and looked back at him once. He waved as he made sure the kayaks were secure. A date? With the beautiful woman who had inspired him to attempt holding her hand. It hadn't been a success. But he had initiated that daring venture. And that felt like a win.

Had she been nervous about calling it a date? And then maybe a little excited?

Who was Saralyn Martin-soon-to-be-Hayes? And would he walk off this island the same man after getting to know her better? Did he want to be the same man?

No, no he did not.

CHAPTER FIVE

WAS CHANGING INTO a lace-trimmed tank top and tying the silk scarf about her bikini-bottom-clad hips dressing up for a date? Yes, island style. And no, she did not allow herself to feel guilty about it. Having a little fun with the only other occupant here on the island? What was wrong with that? It was just dinner. Wasn't like she planned to seduce him, lure him into her world and then marry the guy.

Saralyn paused before the convection oven where the dinners heated, startled by her thoughts. Marry him? She'd just gotten out of a marriage that had been ten years too long. She would never marry again.

She shook her head. That was a lie. She had no qualms about falling in love and possibly marrying again. She liked being in a relationship. But it was far too early to start thinking long-term. First and foremost, she sought someone with whom she could walk through life. Hand in hand.

"It's just dinner," she admonished her flighty thoughts that tended to put her heroes and heroines together too quickly and then they were in love before the first third of the story ended. Never enough conflict. It was something she focused on and had learned to stretch that conflict out through the story.

She and David had no conflict. Save the fact he shouldn't even be here. That he was treading on her own private escape. And that he was fifteen years younger than her and too handsome for a simple, slightly pudgy ghost like her.

Sighing, she shook her head again. Think positive! "This will be fun."

As she took the meals out of the oven, David wandered in with a bottle of wine and— Shoot, he was wearing a shirt.

"Have a seat! You've got perfect timing. The food is ready."

"And so is the wine." He popped the cork and poured their goblets before sitting.

"I love the meal delivery system you offer here." Saralyn set a plate of grilled shrimp with a mango kiwi salsa before him. "For someone who hates to cook elaborate meals, I feel like a chef warming them up."

"It's a popular option, though half our guests do opt for the chef. Marcel LeDoux is a good friend of mine. He used to be our family chef and fed me every day I was growing up."

"That's remarkable that you hired him to work here for you."

"I spent a lot of time in the kitchen when I was a kid and learned a lot over the years observing Marcel and his wife. She was our housekeeper. They were so in love. Made me understand what love could really be like."

"Didn't you know?"

David bowed his head. That felt like a confession, and he appeared as though he hadn't expected those words to leave his mouth so easily. She could relate. The guarded hero.

He lifted his head and added, completely ignoring her curiosity, "Marcel is also an amazing drink master. Larger groups will keep him on for party nights. He may be pushing seventy, but the old man can assume DJ duties in a pinch. You know there's a sound system throughout the island?"

"I do, but I haven't tried it. So I could put on some tunes and dance my way around the beach?"

"Of course. Connect your phone to it and you're off to a beach tango."

"I'll give that a try next time I have my phone out. I like the box. Out of sight, out of mind. It's an essential part of the whole vacation milieu."

She sat next to him, very aware he'd dodged her question about love. Too soon, she admonished inwardly. This was a friendly dinner not a seduction.

Comfortable with his presence now, she couldn't imagine that she'd initially been upset over him being on the island. On the other hand, she had every right to protest a man trying to move in on her peace and quiet.

"I've never tried this dish, so here goes..." A bite melted on her tongue. Subtle lemon and a spice she couldn't name enhanced the flavor but didn't hide it. Add to that the sharp tang from the fruit. "This is amazing."

"Right? These are much tastier than the mackerel I made for you the other night. Entire schools of them swim around the mainland. They never seem to come close enough to the island, though, to spear them."

"Wait, you caught those fish with a spear?"

"How else to do it?"

"A fishing rod and bait?"

"Ha! That's cheating. I prefer the challenge of spearfishing."

"I get that about you. It's your inventor's brain that constantly needs the challenge. What other challenges do you enjoy? I suspect you travel the world adventuring and living the big life."

"I think you've mistaken me for one of your romance heroes."

His steady stare mimicked one of those heroes perfectly.

Oh, Saralyn, do not fall into that smolder.

"I'm not so interesting," he said. "And I avoid the big life, as you put it. I do play water sports and the occasional game of billiards. And I travel. Have a home in Greece. But my life is small. I work very hard to keep it so."

"That's unexpected. I would think a man with unlimited income would live in a castle, drive a fleet of cars, wear expensive suits and, well... where's your girlfriend while you are hiding on a remote island?"

She'd done it. She'd snuck in that question. Because really, a man as handsome and rich as David Crown had to be taken. Yet she'd noticed he had made a move to hold her hand earlier. It had startled her so much all she could do was cling to the swing rope. Much as she would have enjoyed holding his hand, it had felt sudden. Even, daring. Like standing on the edge of a cliff and wondering if she could manage the fall. Because hand-holding led to dating. And much as they'd labeled this dinner a date, she hadn't dated in, oh, so long. However to begin again?

"No girlfriend," he said through a bite of pineapple. "Haven't dated in half a year. I've been too busy."

"With the thing that you said you had to get away from?"

"Yes, the lawsuit. About the blanket. I prefer not to talk about it. But it has consumed my time."

"Sounds like your tropical island escape was necessity."

"My shoulders have already dropped and my gut has stopped churning. But I'm going to give you some credit for that. Your laugh..." He forked in a bite of shrimp, then winked at her.

Saralyn sipped her wine to disguise her sigh. The compliment zoomed straight to her core and spun it about in a heady rise of desire. And no girlfriend? She had read and written far too many stranded-on-a-tropical-island romances to know how this could go. Yet those couples were always close in age and generally spent the entire three hundred pages having sex like bunnies.

They had, after all, made a movie about just that.

Her life had changed with the divorce. And her body had changed since menopause had landed. While she was glad to wave goodbye to monthly cramps, the uneasy feeling that she would dry up and lose all desire had settled in. Logically, she knew that wasn't true. She'd done the research. But illogically, there were days she felt like an old hag waiting for the village young'uns to come ask for her wise advice while she cackled at them.

How to even make the first step toward dating again? It had been over twenty years since she had dated or touched, kissed, and made love to anyone but Brock.

The very thought of dating flashed her back to those uncertain teenage-angst years. Yet at the same time, teenage fascination with all things to do with kissing, touching and even more hovered around the edges of that angst. Only this time the fascination had matured and knew what, where and how to get the satisfaction it craved. And that scared her more than a first kiss in the backseat of a cherry-red 1970s Camaro.

Out the corner of her eye she realized David had propped his hand against his chin. His gaze pinned her with an unthreatening curiosity. An invigorating flash of warmth bloomed in her chest. And she knew darn well it was not a hot flash.

"What?" she asked.

"There you go. Lost again. That writer thing?"

More like an unsure-woman thing. "It is."

"What plot are you concocting right now? A romance?" He waggled a brow, which wasn't so much silly as a devastating arrow right to her libido. "Or a murder mystery where the machete-wielding hero finds the heroine sprawled on the beach, drowned, but for the ligature marks around her neck?"

"Wow, you've given that one some thought. Do I need to be worried?"

"No. I watch far too much of the mystery channel. It's my white noise when I'm at home. Promise I won't strangle you."

"Whew! I'm safe from strangling, but what about drowning?"

He lifted a brow, giving her a moment of heart-stopping concern, then shook his head. "I don't want to kill you, Saralyn, I want to kiss you."

Her mouth dropped open. She had the thought that at the very least she hadn't had any food in it. *Like some kind of silly fumbling teenager.* With heartbeats thundering, she closed her mouth and handled his surprising announcement with as much tact as a woman who had been touch-and-love-starved for years could manage. By stalling.

"You want very much."

Inwardly wincing, she mentally kicked herself for that idiotic reply. Of course, a kiss was on the table! But she didn't know how to do this. Flirting. It had been far too long since she'd felt desirable in a man's eyes.

She set down her fork. "Sorry."

"What for? I do want a lot. You are an exquisite woman, Saralyn. You should require very much from a man. And I should have to meet those requirements and expectations if I'm even to have a chance."

"A chance at what?"

"That kiss."

One that would explode her world in so many ways. Good, bad and—no, not at all ugly. And not even bad. But a little unsure. She suddenly felt bouncy and giddy. Like that teenager sitting beside her crush, wondering if he did make a move, if she would know how to respond. How to kiss him? It had been so long since she'd had a good and proper kiss. One that curled her toes. Colored her thoughts with poetic verse. Shot straight to her erogenous zones.

Here sat a man fifteen years younger than her asking to kiss her. Perhaps it was a test? To see if he liked kissing an older woman? Did he have a thing for older women? So, that was his game.

Should it matter? Probably not. Maybe? Oh!

"There she goes again." David took her finished plate and walked around to the sink to rinse them off. "I want to learn to navigate that industrious brain of yours."

No one had ever said a nicer thing to her. Because her brain was busy and industrious and constantly working. Sometimes to her detriment.

Just be in the moment, Saralyn.

"It's gotta be fascinating inside there," he added.

"Or maybe a madhouse populated with esoteric research, myriads of crazy characters, and only a few real dreams and desires."

He sat at the table again and met her gaze. Soft caring in those whiskey browns. And a certain daring. "I'm going to make learning your dreams and desires my goal. And I'm a man who is known for attaining his goals."

"You already know my dream."

"To have a lovely escape on a tropical island. You see? I'm halfway to the goal already. Now, for your desires." He tapped the plate on which sat a small chocolate truffle cake. "Dessert?"

Saralyn preferred kissing David as the dessert. But her heart tugged her back from that adventure. Slow and cautious. "Please."

She'd not answered his question about the kiss. But neither had she refused it. David had surprised himself by outright asking. Normally he was more suave when pursuing a woman. And that he had seamlessly gone from being cordial and friendly to the island guest who had requested privacy to wanting to kiss her didn't so much surprise him as warn him against making a misstep. He didn't want to push her away.

Because he would like that kiss. Saralyn was the most attractive woman he'd met in a long

time. As much inside as outside. Even though
her insides seemed to be a crazy mess of distracted thoughts about her work and self-effacing
thoughts about her body.

He could make her comfortable. Or he'd try.
He liked that she was a challenge, not like the
women who were eager to jump into bed with
him simply because—well, because he was rich
or handsome. He could read those women like a
book. And not a very interesting book. He liked
the mystery of Saralyn. And he intended to savor
every page of her story she allowed him to read.

"Let's take the rest of this bottle out onto the
veranda." He grabbed the wine bottle.

Goblet in hand, Saralyn led him to the vast
planked veranda that curved along the beach side
of the villa. It offered ample seating and space
for a party. Tiny fairy lights were strung across
the entirety and the furniture was wide, abundant
and cushy. A circular electric fireplace mastered
the center. With a voice command, the fire ignited and flames danced atop the colored glass
in shades of violet, blue and green. With another
command, David set the tropical-themed instru-
mental music to a low volume.

Saralyn sat on the sofa beneath a palm frond
and tugged up her legs beside her. That move of
placing her legs tight to her body felt as if she
was putting distance between them.

Fair enough. That wouldn't dissuade him from this evening's goal of a kiss.

David sat on the wood floor before the sofa, his back to the edge of the thick padded cushion and his shoulder but inches from her knee. Stretching out his legs he crossed his ankles. From the moment he stepped foot on the island, he never wore shoes. He'd done research on grounding and how the body's innate electrical system recharged by walking with bare feet on soil, grass or sand. Never did he feel so relaxed back home in Manhattan where his shoes tread concrete, carpeting and asphalt.

"Is that the same bird I asked about earlier?" she asked of the soft twittering in the trees behind them.

"It's different. There's a bird book inside. The bookshelf offers all kinds of books on tropical flora and fauna."

"I'm on it." She stepped down and he touched her leg.

"Leave it until morning?" he asked. "Or did I accidentally ignite your research mode?"

"You did." She sat again, this time her legs before her instead of tucked on the couch. "But it can wait. This is a beautiful evening. I don't think I've ever seen such clear turquoise water topped by a rose-gold sky. The view is like a photograph. Gorgeous."

He turned and propped an elbow on the sofa to look up at her. "I suspect your research mode is still active."

"Guilty. I'm recording every sunset, every wild plant and bird. The feel of the sand under my feet and the rush of the warm water as I swim through it. Okay, fine. I'll turn off the writer. Just enjoy the evening, Saralyn! I may not get back here in a long time."

"You are welcome on my island anytime."

"That's kind of you, but I am here on my friend's rather generous dime."

"I didn't expect that you would pay. Anytime you want this place for a week? Please let me know."

"I'm not sure what I've done to deserve such a generous offer, but… I'm no fool. I'll remember the offer."

"Smart woman." The whisk of wings overhead alerted them to a flash of brilliant red, blue and emerald. "Parrot," he said. "I do know that one. Only because they can be feisty. Watch your hair if you're eating on the beach."

"Thanks for the warning. Shades of *The Birds* just popped into my brain." She shuddered.

"Do you mind if I join you?"

"Please do. You sitting down there like a puppy is a little disconcerting."

"Disconcerted, eh?" He sat next to her. "Is that a step up or down from aghast?"

"It is a step in the lesser direction from aghast."

"Then, it seems I'm growing on you." He stretched an arm across the back of the sofa, behind her shoulders, but didn't touch her. Slow and easy. She may flee at any moment. Though he sensed her relaxation as she settled against the cushions and smiled at him. "Let's do some get-to-know-each-other questions."

"Oh, please, no favorite colors or pastimes."

"What's wrong with turquoise?" he asked in mock protest.

"Nothing at all. But if we're going to get to know one another better, we need to do a deep dive. And I have the perfect first question."

"Hit me."

She wriggled on the couch, finding joy in her conspiratorial advancing of the plot. "What book are you currently reading?"

Really? Nice. "Well played. Not only do you learn a title from that question, but you also discern that I do actually have a current read. Which, I suspect, will please you."

"Immensely."

"Current read is nonfiction," he said. "I go back and forth between fiction and non. While I can't rattle off the title and author's name I can tell you it's about the Victorian internet."

"What? That's…not right?"

"Oh, it is," he said with a delightfully evil tone. "Or, that historical period's version of the internet. The book details the creation and spread of the first telegraph system across the world. It's something I'm interested in since the Crown family's fortune was built on investments in those very first underground cables that were laid for the telegraph system."

"Really? I guess it was a sort of internet back then. Connecting people through technology. And your family helped to create it?"

"My great-greats had a hand in furthering the communications industry. From the telegraph and Morse code to the telephone and now the internet. The Crowns have always invested in communications and information technology. Look out AI, we're on it! Which, I'll tell you right now, made me a trust fund baby. That's not news. The media is always putting that label before my name like it means something."

"It doesn't?"

"Eh. It means the money came easy to me. And people judge me by that. I've never rested on my guaranteed-income laurels. From my first lemonade stand to selling Marcel's amazing brownies to my classmates at lunch, to fixing their electronic devices and showing the girls how to adjust their privacy settings to keep out hackers, I had to make my own money."

"As a fellow creative soul, I understand the need to work and constantly learn, and to be self-sufficient."

"You get me."

"Some of you, anyway. I would never say no to a trust fund, though."

David laughed. "I've known nothing else. And I do understand I am privileged."

"You don't act like it. But even if you did, what matters is your interaction with others. You seem kind and genuinely interested in...well, people." She looked aside, pressing the wine goblet to her lips. Feeling a little flush? Yes, he was interested in her. And she had picked up on that. He wasn't fishing in uninterested waters. "That book sounds good. I'd like to read it."

"I'll text you the title if you send me your number."

"I'll do that next time I touch my phone."

"So what book are you currently reading?" he asked.

"I generally have three, four or more books going at one time," she said. "A couple fiction, a few nonfiction. Some hard copies, as well as digital. Always research books."

"Which one rises to the top lately?"

"I've discovered a new author who writes hilarious historical-adventure romances. Superfun stuff that reminds me of the old Dick Van Dyke movies with the crazy characters that burst into song and have special abilities. And the romantic banter is first-rate."

"A little *Mary Poppins*? A little *Chitty Chitty Bang Bang*?"

"I love that you are into the oldies but goodies. Every child should be raised on such wonderful stories."

"I watched them in French," he said. "Reading the subtitles. From Marcel's personal library. I spent a lot of time in the den staring at those old movies. I wanted to read Marcel's books, but alas, I may have picked up a few French words over the years, but I can't read or speak it."

"Oh, *désolée*," she said consolingly.

He recognized the word for *sorry*. "You speak French?"

"Not at all," she said on a chuckle. "I have an arsenal of about five words that I use, and not always correctly. Many of my heroes tend to be French. I mean, come on, that language is like music. So sexy."

"Tell me about some of the books you've written. Might I have read them?"

"The ghostwritten stories are off-limits. I can't reveal that information. Because if I did, I'd have to kill you."

"Right, I forgot about that. But have you written for major names? Celebrities?"

"Most likely."

"Oo, you are tight with the details. Okay, I won't push. Maybe. Well, I'm curious now. Have you written anything under your own name?"

"Two books when I first started writing. One was an over-the-top paranormal romance with vampires, ghosts and time travel, rock 'n' roll and major home renovations."

"And the kitchen sink?"

"I did have a kitchen-sink scene in there as well."

David laughed. And she joined him slapping a hand on his thigh, which he felt she didn't notice but he certainly did. The contact was instantly electrifying. The connection started at her fingertips, zinged along his thigh and inserted itself into his nervous system, whooshing all the way up to his cortex. Basically, it made him very aware of his sexual needs. And fast.

"The other was my attempt at a comedy romance," she said, completely unaware of his distraction. "I'm not so good with the one-liners and pratfalls. I'm best with drama and monsters. Toss in a good heist and I am all over that."

"I'd expect the opposite from what I know of you. You're light and so bright. What is it about monsters that attracts you?"

"I like vampires and werewolves because I can create their world and control them within it. And I know they're not real, so it's fun to play with the possibilities of situating them in the real world. Unlike the serial killer books that I avoid like the plague. I don't like being scared by reality."

Neither did he. He'd never been a fan of horror movies and the serial killer stuff. Real life could be much scarier than fantasy.

A flash of light off in the ocean distracted his attention from her voice and his wandering libido. Locals from the mainland Jet Skiing? They never came too close to the island.

"Can I get a copy of those two books?"

"They're out of print."

"Well, since you can't reveal your ghostwriting oeuvre, you'll have to write another under your name so I can read it. Saralyn Hayes, right?"

"Yes, I'll put that request on my list."

"I think it's already on your list but you're afraid to make it reality."

"I think you presume too much about my capabilities in general."

"I doubt it."

He studied her profile. With her hair pulled back into a loose ponytail, her cheekbones glimmered under the glow of the lights strung along the veranda. This woman had not lived five decades. She was utter goddess material. On the other hand, she wore a certain wisdom, a confidence that could only come from walking through the years and learning and witnessing the world. She wasn't a flighty, selfish young thing that believed a person's actions only mattered if recorded and posted on a thirty-second video. If he never dated one of those sorts again, he'd be happier for it.

"Now who's slipped into a random brain freeze?" she teased.

"Guilty. I was thinking about that kiss again."

"Oh." Her entire body tensed. She rubbed a palm along her arm closest to him. However, she relaxed as quickly. "Were you?"

To sit here and discuss a kiss felt awkward, despite his very alert desire. And yet to simply lean in and take one from her didn't feel right. Never had he been so conflicted about a kiss. It had to be right. It had to not offend, but also to even think such a thing spoiled whatever pleasure might be gained from it.

Saralyn set her goblet on the table beside the sofa. With a twist of her waist, she turned to face him. Her smile grew biggest in her eyes. Subtly seductive? Yes, please. With only the slightest hesitation, she ran her fingers through her hair and pushed it over a shoulder. The move teased at the nerve endings in David's body that were already ultrahoned for the slightest beckon. He could feel her all over him though they didn't touch. And she smelled like the flowers growing throughout the island, with a hint of the mango that had seasoned dinner.

"I'm not sure how to do this," he confessed. "I don't want to impose. I don't want to presume anything about…us. I don't want you to think I'm taking advantage of you."

"That's a lot of don'ts."

Yes, wasn't it? Not his style. Was he flustered by a woman? Get over it, man!

"But as well, you are like stars in the sky far from the city, Saralyn. It is a marvel to look at you, and I can't stop looking at you. And I want to get close, reach up and…"

She moved in closer. "And?"

A flash of light—too close—made them both look toward the beach.

"What is that?" she asked. "Some kind of speedboat?"

"Jet Skiers. I noticed them earlier. Looks like they are heading toward the dock. Probably tourists unaware of the island's boundaries." He stood, not happy to have decreased their proximity. "I'm going to talk to them. Inform them this is a private island." When he turned to see if she would respond, he noticed her catch a yawn against her wrist. "Getting late?"

"It's been an adventurous day. I think I am ready to turn in. Thank you for the date. It was a lovely evening."

A loud rev of the Jet Ski turned his focus back to the beach. "Sorry, I'll get them to leave. Good night, Saralyn. See you tomorrow?"

"I'll make breakfast if you're interested."

"Always!"

He marched away toward the beach with a glance to the sky speckled with copious stars. Tonight, he'd almost kissed a star.

CHAPTER SIX

THIS MORNING AS she was getting dressed, Saralyn blew her reflection a kiss. Both the bikinis she'd packed were currently getting a refresh in the dryer, so she donned a pair of linen shorts and a floaty camisole. She pulled her hair back into a ponytail, then decided against it and went with a loose chignon with some strands down around her face. A romantic look.

For a romantic mood.

She'd almost kissed David last night! Almost. Darn those Jet Skiers. Yet, also, whew!

In the moment when they'd been sitting so close and had been *this close* to a kiss, her nerves had zinged beneath her skin. She'd tried to act as though she had it all together. *Grown woman here. Totally in for the seduction, for the kiss.*

And she had been!

But when they'd gotten so close that it had almost happened, a voice inside her head had yelled, *What are you doing? Do you even know how to do this? Are you crazy? Thinking you can just*

*make out with the handsome man? The younger
man. The hero you don't deserve. Because you
don't know how to keep a man, to make him so
happy he won't look elsewhere.*

Saralyn sneered at her reflection. Stupid inner
voice. She had every right to kiss any man she
desired. And it was about time to start acting on
her newly emerging beliefs.

Look at that woman in the mirror. Knocking
on the door to her fiftieth birthday. Divorced.
Squeezed through the emotional wringer. Not so
sure of herself. And yet, she had almost kissed
the sexy billionaire.

"You almost did," she said to her now-approving
reflection. "And next time? You will."

Grabbing her sun hat, she strolled out to the
kitchen and remembered she'd invited David for
breakfast. The prepared meal was a quiche, so
she popped that in the oven to warm, then mixed
up a pitcher of sangria. White wine, a hit of rum,
plenty of fresh pineapple, orange slices and cher-
ries. Yes, she was drinking in the morning. Because she could.

Remembering the sound system, she retrieved
her phone from the Faraday box and connected
to the Wi-Fi. Clicking on her *Good Vibes* play-
list, a soft melody drifted in from the veranda
speakers. She adjusted the volume lower. If the

island were wired throughout, she was probably entertaining the entire place.

All of a sudden David danced up onto the veranda, singing the uplifting chorus. "I love this song!" he called as he walked inside and bowed grandly before her. A knightly gesture offered her a huge purple flower blossom. "For you, my lady."

"That's gorgeous." She took it and sniffed the deep violet bloom. Definitely not one of the sweet-smelling blossoms that had been perfuming the air.

"What's wrong?" He leaned forward to sniff the flower she offered. "Nope. That's not good at all." He took it and tossed it outside onto the sand. "Sorry."

"No worries. It was the thought that counts. I made sangria. And the quiche should be warm."

They went through the motions of plating the food and pouring drinks, dancing around one another, but not quite touching. The air between them was different now. More sensually charged but also a little tense. Saralyn wondered if he'd try to kiss her. Should *she* try to kiss him? For as alive as being around him made her feel, she didn't want to push a good thing and risk destroying it. Best to play it by ear and follow his lead.

Was that really the way a woman who intended

to own her life and take control acted? Shouldn't she be more in charge? Grasp hold of her destiny and shape it to her command?

I am woman! Hear me roar!

David's finger snap near her face startled her into the moment. "Did I do it again?" she asked.

"Yes. Has the hero slain the dragon yet?"

"No, but he has captured the heroine's interest. They have a lot of pages ahead of them before any dragon slaying can occur."

"Good to know. I'll make sure the hero keeps his sword sheathed for a while. Uh…" He smirked and shook his head.

Saralyn considered what he'd just said and how it could allude to something sexual. Awkward? No, actually kind of cute that he was playing along with her mental mind bursts.

"I'm sure the heroine will appreciate the knight's caution," she reassured. "Of course, anything can happen in a romance. There are always twists to be had."

He met her glass with a *ting*. The sangria was sweet. With a wince at the surprising alcohol content, he said through a gasp, "I also like a good twist." He broke into a twisting-hip dance move. "See what I did there?"

"You're absolutely hilarious."

"Not so much, but I appreciate the rousing

endorsement. Want to learn how to spear fish today?"

"Can I take notes?"

"Only if you don't mind them getting soggy."

"I'll keep mental notes. As long as you clean and cook whatever we catch."

"If you manage to catch a fish, I will be happy to take care of the dirty work that follows. That is, if I survive this drink and don't spear my own foot in a drunken haze."

"Cheers!" She tinged his glass again and he took another swallow as she finished off her sangria.

Yes, she was feeling her oats this morning. Or something that resembled a flirty, fidgety, flustery need to get on with the shaping of her life—and to do that shaping alongside David.

Later, after David had retrieved a couple spears and a line with hooks for wrangling their catch, they waded out to his favorite fishing spot and plopped down on a car-sized flat rock that served as a makeshift dock. Swim trunks his only clothing, he dangled his bare feet in the azure water and explained the fish usually arrived not long after the sun reached its peak in the sky.

"You ever fish before?" He leaned his palms back on the rock and turned his face to the sun, closing his eyes. "When you were growing up in Iowa?"

Saralyn would never tire of marveling over his physique, the gleaming bronze muscles and those soft dark hairs that glittered with water droplets. Every movement shifted those muscles tectonically and created a new sculpture for her to admire.

What had he asked? Right. Focus!

"Dad used to take us ice fishing. That involved me and Mom shivering in the corner of the icehouse watching the little portable TV while Dad manned the fishing line. I was never much into winter activities. The snowshoe trip to the frozen lake was misery to me."

"Thus your reason for heading to sunny California?"

"Pretty much. But also, my girlfriend Juliane suggested I move in with her so she could afford the rent, and I liked the idea of being so close to the entertainment industry."

"Lots of book agents in Los Angeles?"

"Enough. More script agents and movie producers. I've never had the desire to write a screenplay. Well…until…"

David rolled onto his side to give her his complete attention. She'd not intended to let that slip. She was contracted with a gag order. Not even Brock had been aware of her connection to the movie. Thank goodness. That information had been kept out of the divorce settlement.

"That 'until' sounded so damn intriguing," David said. "I might risk you having to kill me because I need you to spill the beans."

If the man had been plain and perhaps her age, just another Joe in the world and not the super-attractive charmer who made her insides dance like a teenager crushing hard, she may have easily brushed off his query. She'd been doing it for years. Friends often tried to guess at who she wrote as, or what celebrities' stories she had written. Her lips were always sealed. Yet, she had suggested Juliane choose this specific island as her vacation spot.

You have to see where that movie was filmed. It looked so romantic!

Juliane would never have known it was *the* island.

Only now. If ever she'd had a niggle of desire to reveal her great secret it blossomed to a tickle. And she'd never been good at surviving a proper tickle.

David waggled a brow. The move lured her gaze to his deep brown eyes which held a mischievous grin in the irises. That implied tickle made her wriggle within her clothes. She'd been a good girl all these years. Kept her mouth shut. In ways that had devastated her emotionally. Wasn't it time to let out the merest hint? To take back some of her independence?

"I won't press," he started, "because I'm sure it's in your contract, but—"

"Let's just say I've written a novel for a major author, whose publisher then optioned that story and it was made into a movie. Recently."

His approving nod fed her need for notice, to be seen. She wouldn't be human if she denied how good it might feel to see her name listed in the credits for a movie. Her words on the big screen! What author didn't want to claim as much?

"Anything I've seen?" he prompted.

Saralyn compressed her lips. She'd said too much. And if David ever let it slip… Well, what could they do to her? Wasn't like she was receiving royalties from the movie or the book. The worst the publisher could do was never buy from her again. And that would make her decision much easier.

"It was set on a tropical island," she blurted out.

A flip-flop in her gut warned her not to say more. Yet, there it was…*tickle, tickle*. Wasn't it time she received *some* credit for her work? If one person in the world could know… It wouldn't be fame, exactly, but it might give her a taste of the feeling she craved.

"And it was filmed on this island," she tossed in quickly.

David sat up, resting an arm on his knee. "*Sex on the Beach*? You wrote that?"

She scrunched up her face and made the slightest nod. She hadn't expected he'd guess it so quickly. Then again, he was the island's owner. Of course, the film company had dealt with him to make the movie.

"That movie was awesome. And I'm not saying that because it was filmed on my island and they paid me a sweet rental fee for the month of filming. Although...whew! It was steamy. You wrote all that sex?"

Suddenly defensive, she lifted her chin. "You don't think I'm capable?"

"Well, sure, but... Damn, Saralyn Hayes. That was one hot story."

His eyes drifted over her body from head to as far down as she dared follow his gaze. Considering her on completely new terms after learning she had written an erotic story? It didn't offend her so much as lift her confidence. Hell yes, she could write the sexy stuff. No research necessary, boys, she knew her subject. And it had been made into a major movie.

"Nice," he added.

"All right." She picked up the spear from the rock beside her and pointed the tip near his chest. "Now's the part where I have to kill you."

She was killing him with her easy sensuality. David felt sure she wasn't even aware of it. The soft glint in her brown eyes. The natural rose shimmer of her slightly curled lips. And that earthy chestnut hair that spilled in waves over her bare shoulders. Her movements, a glide of a bare leg along the other, a curl of her fingers about the back of her ear, were naturally sensual. When had a death threat ever felt so seductive?

He held up his hands in surrender. "Whatever you do, make it quick." He tapped his heart. "Right here."

The spear tip hit the water and she laughed. "I could never pull off a murder. Sure, your body may be washed away to sea, but if a billionaire mogul goes missing? Or your body floats onto shore on the mainland? I'd break down and confess the moment a detective asked me my name."

"Good to know I'm safe from murder today."

But as for her seductive sensuality he'd play victim to that every day, all day.

"I promise I won't reveal your secret about *Sex on the Beach*," he said. "I know how binding contracts can be. I think it's cool that you let me in on it. And to know you're the word master behind that movie? Neato."

"Neato? Here I thought I was the older one. Where'd you dig up that word? From the 1970s?"

"Maybe? Attribute to me watching all those old black-and-white television reruns when I was a kid. In addition to Gilligan, the Beaver and Andy Griffith were my babysitters."

"Oh." Her gaze fluttered up to his. And her mood suddenly changed. "I'm sorry. Were your parents not around that much?"

David shrugged it off. Because he sensed a rise of empathy that he wouldn't know how to accept. "No worries."

In truth, his childhood had shaped him in ways he was still struggling with and he wasn't a guy who put his troubles out there for the world to analyze. It was bad enough the trial had done so. He'd been his own worst enemy of late.

"Hey!" He pointed to the water near her feet. "We're in luck."

Saralyn noticed the fish swimming around her legs, their silvery scales glinting the closer they swam to the sun-shimmered surface. She leaned forward on the rock to study the shallow waters. Her hair spilled over a shoulder and David reached to touch…

"Oh, I don't know," she said. He pulled back. "They're so cute. How can I possibly spear one of them?"

"Well, you did eat one the other day."

She bit her lip. "Shoot, I did. And you guys were very delicious," she cooed to the fish shimmering in the water. "Okay, I'm over it." She picked up the spear. "This chick cannot survive on four-star chef meals alone. Let's do this!"

An hour later, David counted three fish on the line. He'd speared all of them. As soon as Saralyn had locked in a perfect aim, she'd pull back and mutter some excuse about the sun glinting on the surface. Understandable. It probably took a certain sanguine thrill to do the deed, and she was far from cold-blooded.

Rather hot-blooded, he suspected. That movie had certainly pushed its R rating to the limits. Whew! Any woman who could write sex like that was— What was he thinking? Writers made up things for a living. That didn't mean she was a sexual dominatrix or had tried all the different positions that had been featured in the movie.

He wasn't interested in sexual gymnastics with Saralyn. Well, sure, but. What really intrigued him was the connection they were forming. She had sunk under his skin and was taking hold in his very being. And he liked the feeling. A lot.

"I've let you down," she said with a gesture to the fish line.

"Not at all. Any more than this and we'd have too much for a meal. I hate to waste."

"You're very good with the spear. You give off caveman alpha-hunter vibes."

He straightened at the compliment. Yes, he

was a hunter of food. A warrior who brought home dinner for his woman. Triumph!

"I know I could have speared that one fish," she added. "And it's not because I don't have the courage. I just…"

Her sigh felt uncomfortable in David's soul. It was heavy with something that he recognized. A need for something ineffable. And yet, he knew exactly what that need was. It was voicing it that would challenge his very bravery and being.

"I should be able to catch my own fish. Prepare my own meal," she said. "I want to not need a man, you know?"

"Thankfully," he bowed to catch her gaze, "we live in modern society and it isn't necessary for you to do such a thing. You can buy fish in a grocery store. Slashing a credit card is still considered fending for yourself."

"I suppose." She would not be convinced.

"So…" He sat next to her and dangled the line of fish in the water. One of the silver-scaled fish still wriggled. "You don't need a man? Because of your divorce? Didn't you say something about liking a man in your life?"

"I did and I do. But I've learned a few things about myself lately. I don't want to rely on a man for basic survival. I want to be able to support myself. To buy all my necessities and do things for myself, like small repairs and changing oil on a car."

"Even I take my car in for the oil change."

"Yes, but it's so simple. You just remove the oil cap, unscrew the oil plug, let the oil drain, then replace the plug and fill 'er up."

"You have done some research."

"It was for a celebrity bio. He was a former auto mechanic. I research heavily to understand my subject. Anyway, I'm not saying men are bad. I like men. You guys are nice to have around."

"*Useful.* Wasn't that the word you used?"

"Yes, but in the most complimentary manner."

"Good to know you've not given up on us all. Will you…tell me about the marriage? Living the Hollywood lifestyle. It must have been crazy. But if it's too personal…"

She pulled up her legs to her chest and wrapped her arms around them, propping her chin on her knees. A protective position. Perhaps he shouldn't have asked, but he was interested in learning anything she would give him. He couldn't step back now. That almost-kiss had changed things. It had made him realize that since that first day he'd walked up to her on the beach, he'd wanted to get to know everything he could about the beautiful woman in the bright bikini whose laughter woke up his soul.

"I told you my husband is an actor," she finally said. "He plays Cave Kendall on *Paradise Place*. One of the last remaining soap operas still on television."

"Cave? Seriously? Where do they get those names?"

"Right? I once named a character Stone. Geography-related names tend to be popular for alpha males."

"I'll keep that in mind. Perhaps I should name my first-born Valley? Or Granite!"

"Oh, I like Granite. Very commanding and stoic. I would call him Gran for short!"

She laughed and her body tilted against his, their shoulders nudging. The sweep of her hair teased him to touch it, which he did, unobtrusively. She didn't notice. And when she pressed her chin back onto her knees, he kept the tip of her hair between his fingers. A strand to connect them. A lifeline he wanted to breathe through.

"Anyway," she continued, "I was introduced to Brock, that's my ex-husband's name, at a book release party. I knew he was an actor, and with stars in my eyes, I fell for his practiced charm. Then, I never believed it was an act. He had a way of making me feel special, like I was the only woman in the room. That lasted for years. But now I know it was… Well." She turned her head to face him. "I can hope some of it was real."

Should he offer reassurance? Didn't feel right. Whatever she felt about that long relationship was valid and hers to own. So instead he twirled the tip of her hair about his finger and waited for her to continue.

"Our romance was whirlwind. After a month, he proposed. We married three months later. Initially, I accompanied him to all the parties, premieres and media junkets. I quickly learned that I was not comfortable with the attention. It was rather seamless, me slipping into the background and claiming a headache or writing deadline to get out of another party. He eventually stopped asking me to go along with him."

David had never married or had a relationship that lasted longer than six months, so he could not relate to the mechanics of such a union. Certainly, his parents had never been around often enough to model what a loving relationship could look like. All he knew was from what he'd witnessed by watching Marcel and his wife. But he had learned enough about Saralyn to understand her need for quiet and calm.

Yet hadn't she said something about *seeking* the spotlight? To be known? Perhaps she hadn't thought that far ahead. How could a woman who was a self-proclaimed ghost be comfortable with the delving and merciless media spotlight?

"When a publisher asked Brock to write his

autobiography, he looked to me," she said. "My agent was gangbusters about how easy the job would be. I had already ghostwritten half a dozen autobiographies about celebrities."

"Doesn't the definition of *autobiography* mean it was written by the person it's about?"

"Yes, but you'd be surprised how many are ghostwritten. Just because you're a celebrity does not make you a writer. Though certainly I know of many self-written autobiographies that are excellent. So, I agreed and it was an easy write. In two months, I had drafted out the entire manuscript."

"Is that fast?"

"It is for me. Generally, I take nine months to a year to write an autobiography. That includes research time. I saved the research on Brock for after the draft so I would have an outline of research points. I'd planned to sit down with him one weekend and interview him about any outstanding items. But first, I verified my facts and details. A stupid part of me looked up some of his emails, thinking I could verify dates of some notable parties. I never dreamed I'd fall into a rabbit hole that would reveal his affairs."

She bowed her head against her knees. "I was able to put together dates and events. And... God help me, one night, I searched his phone calls. The fool never erased those from his phone or his texts. That confirmed my suspicions. I stopped counting after six women over an eight-year period. There could have been more. I know there were. He would never confirm that for me during the divorce proceedings."

"I'm so sorry, Saralyn."

"Me too." She sighed heavily. "But I brought it on myself by not accompanying him to the events and parties. I should have made more of an effort. I wasn't the woman my husband needed."

That she blamed herself angered him. "A wife shouldn't have to babysit her husband. A marriage should mean something. Vows are made to be kept. They are not guidelines."

"Right? I took my vows seriously. Well, it's over now." She tickled her fingers across the water's surface. "I've moved on. Or I will when I return home. I have to be out of the house by autumn."

"And you're not sure where you will land?"

"Nope. My girlfriend Mabel, who lives in my hometown in Iowa, offered me her extra room until I find a permanent place. But I don't want to do that. Especially not if it sees me staying through the winter. And my mom lives there as well. I would like to be close to her but again… Winter."

"The cold does tend to be cold." David could

handle the New York winters for the reason that he rarely spent time outdoors. Running on an indoor track and walking from valet stand to the sidewalk did not challenge a man's physical endurance for extreme weather.

"I'll get my act together," she said. "I've been telling myself I'm fine and… I think I am. I'm forming new grooves."

"You're a strong woman, Saralyn. You can have any life you desire."

"Bold words coming from a man who doesn't have to worry about money."

He wasn't sure how that related to the topic but he understood how people viewed him. He had a lot of money. He could literally have any life he desired. "I earned that money."

"I know you did. That was a rude thing to say. I'm just in a different financial situation from you. Don't worry. I'm not destitute. I'll be able to buy myself a home and set up a retirement account. Then, if I can keep selling my writing, I'll be set. But that's the dilemma. *Can* I sell under my own name? It would bring in more money than ghostwriting does. Whew! I can't believe I spilled all that to you."

"I'm glad you trusted me to do so. It's the real you speaking now. Stepping out of your ghostly raiment."

"That's very poetic."

"I have my moments." He caught her grin and winked.

"You are a charmer."

"I'll take it. But it doesn't come naturally."

"I'd guess differently. You have a stunning smolder."

"So I've been told."

"Well, keep it holstered. Right now I think we need to take care of those fish before they suffer too much. That one is still alive!"

Sensing she needed a subject change, David hopped off the rock and gestured she should lead the way. Together they waded back to the beach.

"Thank you," she said, twisting her toes into the fine sand. "For listening. I rarely talk about the divorce. Not even with my mom. It felt good to put it out there."

She made a move, lifting her arms to perhaps hug him. And like a lightning strike, the past echoed in David's brain. *You wretched thing!* Instinctually, he stepped back from Saralyn. The line of fish slapped against his calf. He immediately regretted the impulsive move. But he had no emotional structure with which to make it right.

"Oh," she said, dropping her arms. "Sorry. I was just going to hug you in thanks, but—"

"No worries," he rushed out. "I'm…not big on hugs."

She tilted her head. Obviously thinking, *the*

inventor of a blanket that hugs a person isn't big on hugs? It was never a conversation he was comfortable having. So he jiggled the line of fish and started walking away, "I'll see you in a bit! White wine goes best with these fellas!"

He caught her wave as he turned and hastened his pace.

Idiot! He'd just made a wrong step. Metaphorically pushed her away when he had wanted to pull her in and...

But that pulling-in part always baffled him. Much like holding hands did. He knew how a hug worked. And that people utilized hugs as a means of thanks, of comfort, a way of acknowledging friendship, of signifying intimacy. He'd been hugged a few times in his life. Quickly. Awkwardly. It always made him stiffen up and wish he were anywhere else.

The one time he had tried to hug his mom—that had ended disastrously. *You wretched thing!*

How to move beyond that voice that arose every time he considered the act of hugging another person? That's all he'd ever wanted in his life. A hug.

CHAPTER SEVEN

WHILE THEY WERE eating grilled fish and honey-glazed pineapple, the rain started to pick up. David explained the tropical storms were infrequent but could sometimes grow windy and wild.

"We should close the windows and doors," he said as they finished drying the dishes.

"Batten down the hatches?"

"Aye, aye!"

Saralyn smiled to herself, even as her nerves took a leap. If she was going to be stormed in, she was thankful to have David here with her. Had she been alone on this island, and if anything had gone wrong, or the wind blew off the roof, she certainly wouldn't have known how to deal with it on her own. Another reason why she would never completely swear off having a good man in her life.

David rushed around the villa, securing each room, and returned clapping his hands in a job well done. "All battened, captain. No need to be distraught."

She laughed at his almost supernatural power

at determining her mood. "I am relieved that you are here. I love thunderstorms but the wind scares me. Will you stick around until the storm stops?"

"What if it rains all night?"

She shrugged. "Slumber party, it is."

His face brightened. "I've never been invited to a slumber party." He plopped onto the sofa, spreading his arms across the back, and put up his feet on the table, fashioned from a twisted tree trunk. "What's involved? Painting each other's nails? Secret confessions? Slam books?"

"Seriously? You know what a slam book is?" Saralyn retrieved a bottle of wine from the fridge. Red, this time. She wasn't big on white, but it had gone well with the meal. "I think those things are considered vintage now."

"Man, I really am getting old."

"Let's not talk about age." She handed him the bottle, a corkscrew, and set down the goblets on the table. "I hereby declare all occupants of this island are classified as ageless."

The cork popped. He poured her a glass. "Hear, hear. Age is just for driver's licenses and colonoscopies."

"Let's also not discuss all the medical procedures one must endure when one reaches a certain age. Here's to long life and ever-flowing wine. You know the resveratrol in the grapes is good for your health?"

"Then, we're drinking this whole bottle." He tilted his goblet to hers.

For a while, they sat listening to the rain, which pattered heavily on the roof and against the three stories of windows. The curved room was incredible. Three stories of windows to capture the beach, sky and tropical foliage. Above the half-circle sofa hung a huge chandelier spiked with foot-long quartz-crystal points that formed a constellation. Outside, the palm trees swished like cancan skirts. The sky darkened, but still a ribbon of rose glimmered through the streaks of rain. It was weirdly romantic, if a person could get beyond the fear of a hurricane.

Saralyn loved a good rainstorm but preferred a gentle one that allowed her to walk outside in raincoat and galoshes. Yet what better houseguest than the man who had walked off the pages of her unwritten romance novel.

Now to start a meaningful conversation. Favorite colors and foods were off the list. Who cared about that stuff? She'd lived enough years to know most people did not change much and that they were set in their ways. And those were the ways she wanted to suss out regarding David Crown.

"We started on important get-to-know-you questions the other day with my book-reading query," she said. "So what's the one question you'd ask a person to get to know them?"

"Ah, that's easy." He tipped his wineglass to hers with a *ting*. "What new thing have you learned today?"

Oh, she liked that one. "Spearfishing!" she announced. "I think it's a good idea to learn something new every day, if you can."

"Agreed. Life has been given to us to be lived. Don't let it get old and rusty."

"We can't avoid the getting-old part."

"I mean, don't let your experiences grow stale and old. Boring. Same old, same old. Learn something new every day."

"Always. Even if it's only on the page."

And by all means, avoid searching your husband's phone records.

She'd learned a tough but necessary lesson. So perhaps a smart woman would move forward with a more discerning idea of what entailed privacy.

"So, you don't have a girlfriend," she blurted. Why bother with small talk? They'd done enough of that. "Why is that? I know you explained about the stress you've been going through with the lawsuit. But I would think a woman in your life would ground you after a long day at the office or laboratory, distract you from the craziness of life."

"Is that how girlfriends are supposed to work? Grounding and distraction? I haven't found one with those particular qualities."

"Maybe you're looking in the wrong places?"

He shrugged. "Eh. I've dated many. They are all in for the big life and are let down when they realize I'm not about the glitz and jet-set lifestyle. I've just never found my person. You know? That one person you don't feel you can go a day without talking to."

"When you put it that way, I'm not sure my ex-husband was my person. We could go days without talking."

"Really? Sounds nightmarish."

"Or just me playing hermit and him living his life despite his marital vows."

"That you are smiling when you say that gives me some hope that you've picked yourself up, dusted yourself off, and—"

"Am getting on with it. Picked up. Dusted off. Now, what's next?"

He turned and tilted his head to study her face. They sat close, knees touching and bodies slouched against the back of the sofa. It was a precious intimacy that didn't scare Saralyn so much as invite her to the next level. Push her to take control of her life and seek her desires.

What *was* next? She was feeling the wine. Relaxing.

"Are you ready to date?" he asked. "I suspect all the single men in Los Angeles must be pounding down your door."

"It's not so easy to begin again," she said while suppressing a sigh. "I did try an online-dating service a month ago." She mocked a shudder.

"That bad?"

"Oh, my goodness, it creeped me out. You've never tried it? Wait, I know the answer. A man of your charm and sex appeal would never need a dating app."

"If you say so."

He knew she was right, so she'd let it go. "I swiftly learned the idea of making a connection with a face on a computer and a few lines of descriptive text doesn't work for me. And the few times I texted a potential guy, they moved quickly to wondering about my favorite sexual position or if I'd be willing to meet them at a hotel. Ugh."

"Hookups are not cool."

"Not at all, and they're not something I'd ever be comfortable with. Making love with a person means something to me. You have to know and trust a person before you…well." She glanced at him shyly now. He nodded, agreeing with her unspoken sentiment. "I mean, I'd love to date again. You men are imminently interesting. And it's not that I fear the next man will be a repeat of Brock. It's that I don't exist in a man-meeting environment. I work from home. Spend innumerable hours sitting before the computer. I don't go to parties. And I lost most of our shared friends with the divorce. So…how to meet a man?"

"How about random encounters while walking your dog and the leashes tangle about your legs?"

Saralyn laughed. "You really do like those older movies, don't you?"

"Love them. But I suspect you're not a dog person?"

"I've not had pets due to Brock's allergies. I hope to someday get a cat."

"Cats are independent, entitled and demanding, but incredibly cool. Perhaps for the great manhunt, you just need to find yourself alone on a tropical island with one of them?"

"Perhaps?" She sipped and lingered with her lips on the slick glass edge.

David's eyes danced in the dim light. And he smelled like rugged races up the side of a mountain only to take a plunge into a refreshing clear ocean. A kiss felt inevitable. But the cliché nudged at her. Forced together by a storm. Sitting together on the sofa. Sharing snippets of their lives with one another. The inevitable was naturally a kiss.

"Wow." He grabbed the bottle and refilled his glass then hers. "You and that wandering brain of yours."

"I know, it's a terrible habit."

"Tell me where you just were?"

Dare she? He probably wasn't aware of the romance tropes and how they played out on the page.

"I mean," he leaned closer, his breath hushing across her cheek "I could guess…"

"I was thinking we could try for that kiss again," she rushed out. "But."

"But?" A slight lift of his chin scored him a point on the seduction scale. Because the angle of his eyes looking down at her put her in a languorous inner sigh that wanted to stretch out and let him drink her in. Yet it was his deep, try-me voice, which spilled over her skin, that took it to the next level. "What's stopping you?"

"Honestly? The cliché of it."

"The…" He gaped. Then ruffled his fingers back through his thick, loose curls as he chuckled. "Is this what dating a writer is like?"

"We're not dating."

"Technically…" He lifted a finger. "We did claim dinner as a date. And right now we *are* flirting."

Saralyn tugged in her lower lip with a tooth. A smile was irresistible. Flirtation had never felt so easy. So natural. Maybe she could try a hand at this dating thing?

"All clichés aside," he said, "you fascinate me, Saralyn. There's always something going on in there." He touched the side of her head, then smoothed his fingers along her hairline. A touch that skittered thrilling shivers over her skin, down her neck and to her breasts. "I want to dive in and swim through it all. Learn the universe of you."

"The universe of me?" Wow. That one did it for her. The man couldn't understand how his words touched all her erogenous zones. How his touch had stirred a warmth that overtook her entire body. And it wasn't a cozy-winter-night's-snuggle warmth but rather a sit-up-and-demand-more kind of touch.

Tempted by his deep voice and poetic sweet nothings, she leaned forward and tapped a finger on his knee. "You may see a vast universe before you, but I'll never be an open book."

She traced her finger along his thigh and up, over the shirt he rarely wore, and pressed her palm over his chest and beating heart. The heat of him seared her senses and she had to repress an audible sigh.

"I like that about you," he said. "Mysterious. Authentic."

"You think?"

"You are." Tucking his curled fingers under hers, he lifted them to kiss her knuckles.

Saralyn sucked in a gasp at the tender touch. When was the last time a man had ever given her such intense and focused attention? *Too long ago.*

The moment felt vast. Truly like the universe. It tingled with promise. Like stars twinkling in the sky. Or the crystals overhead. Desire enveloped her as if an invisible fog overwhelming all.

"Let's be cliché," he whispered. A wink followed. "Just for the fun of it?"

Oh, yes, please.

Saralyn leaned closer, meeting him forehead to forehead. "I'm in."

Their breaths hushed, mingling as they slowly connected. For one ridiculous moment before their lips touched, Saralyn wondered if she should push him away. The answer was a definitive no. She wasn't a silly teenager. This woman knew what she wanted.

Their mouths melted against one another. The heat of him transferring to her and softening her entire being. He couldn't know that she wondered if he would think she was out of practice. It didn't matter because every motion went slowly, learning, allowing her time to rediscover a place she had never visited yet had written about so many times. The hero's kiss. The heroine's sigh. That first moment when finally they connected in a manner that words could never describe. Intense want and need and even a greedy desire seemed to overwhelm. And it felt immense and wondrous and…

Saralyn pulled back. They hadn't moved too

quickly. Just the surprise that she liked it so much, startled her.

"That was…" she said. "I've forgotten how easy it is to get lost in a kiss."

"I'll take that as a good thing?"

"It is. Because once lost, then a person must begin to find themselves."

"I don't know if my kisses can do that for you, but…" He kissed her quickly. "Let's keep at it. You never know what can happen. Or what you'll find."

Like falling for a man fifteen years younger than her? Like allowing herself to get lost and then hoping upon hope that she actually could find something new and exciting in the adventure of David Crown? What if she chased him away as she had done to Brock?

No. They weren't married. They had no vows or commitment to one another.

Maybe she could allow whatever wanted to happen *to happen*. She had accepted this surprise vacation with a determination to return home having found her groove. This could be just the groove she needed.

"I'm in," she whispered.

They kissed, trying different head positions and with soft laughter as they teased fingers along arms, ribs and the smooth underside of a jaw that segued into dark stubble. Eventually they found themselves lying on the sofa. David's hand roamed her body and she didn't protest the exploration. A thumb rubbing her nipple arched her back and she moaned against his hot and full lips. His hips hard against hers could not hide his erection, thick and heavy. She rocked against him but cautioned herself. Sex felt inevitable, but…far too fast. She had only been here a handful of days. And she had meant it earlier when she'd told him making love meant something to her.

Was there anything wrong with enjoying the slow discovery of one another?

When David pulled reluctantly away and studied her gaze beneath the glowing chandelier, she could read his thoughts. He wondered if they might move to the next step. His body certainly alluded that he was ready and willing.

"I'm not sure," she said. She touched his kiss-plump mouth and he kissed her fingers. Slowly. Reverently. "This is moving quickly."

"We can go slower." His lips brushed the base of her neck. A soft hush followed by the tip of his tongue made her gasp. "I'm in no hurry."

"Parts of you may disagree," she offered with a nudge of her hips upward.

"I do have some self-control. Another kiss and then we say goodnight?"

"Sounds like a perfect ending to a perfect evening."

CHAPTER EIGHT

IN THE MORNING, Saralyn decided to check her messages. She'd been here almost a week. And as suspected, her mom had texted her nearly every day despite Saralyn explaining she'd intended to turn off her phone while here.

Just checking in. Are you okay? I heard about a hurricane in the Atlantic Ocean! I hope you're all right.

She texted back that she was in a different ocean entirely and not to worry. Lots of sunshine, sand between her toes, and good story ideas.

She didn't explain that those story ideas involved a sexy, tall, dark-haired man who could kiss a woman back to her teenage years. Her mom would worry if she knew she was on an island alone with a strange man. Lifelong hippie that she was, Sienna Martin was cautious about everything, even walking her small-town main street. Her mom would love for her daughter to move back to Iowa, find a house a few blocks away from her and become settled. And while Saralyn felt some pull to be close to her mother as she aged—she was a vibrant, healthy seventy-five—she knew her mom had excellent health insurance and a boyfriend who doted on her and who was also into daily walking and keeping fit. As well, she owned a small online business selling crystals and yoga mats. Saralyn couldn't ask for a better life for her mom.

Now, to focus on her life. Which was beginning to feel lighter. And promising. Was it the make-out session with David that had her dancing around the kitchen this morning in a bikini as she poured fresh-squeezed orange juice and prepared a bowl of sliced mango and coconut shreds?

Yes. And just thinking that cautioned her. David may make her feel younger, sexy and boost her self-confidence, but a little romance could never be life-changing. Especially when she had a bit more than a week left here on the island.

Well, it *could* be life-changing, but only on the page. She'd been burned romantically, and while she didn't want the divorce to affect the way she viewed any future relationship, the burn marks would never fade.

"Just have fun," she coached herself. "Be yourself. Let loose. No one needs to know about this experiment with kissing a new man. You'll return home and life will go on."

So a fling it was? While Saralyn was not the fling sort of girl, she didn't want to let the opportunity for a connection between her and David slip from her fingers. So why not enjoy herself? David had so many great qualities. He was quiet yet strong. Smart, yet she felt as though they were intellectual equals, which was a refreshing change. They could converse and it didn't have to be light banter about whatever was trending on social media.

Yet there was something he hid from her. She sensed a guarded heart in David Crown. It was in the way he'd avoided a hug and holding hands. What sort of trauma did a person experience that taught them to avoid closeness while also allowing him to kiss and caress her? It was the personal intimacy of the hug that seemed to frighten him. So odd that he'd invented a blanket that did what he most feared.

Perhaps it made sense.

She glanced to the sofa where the blanket had been neatly strewn across one arm. It was too warm to require a blanket; she'd been sleeping with the linen sheets pushed to the end of the bed.

Curiosity prompted her to pick it up. The fabric was light and soft as kitten's fur. She'd expected it to be heavy like those weighted blankets. Wrapping it around her shoulders, she tugged it across her chest and...

"Oh."

The blanket actually did hug her. It conformed to her body. Lightly. Not enough to feel pressure but secure enough to notice the pleasant envelopment.

"Wow," she whispered. "This thing really works."

Easy now to understand how David had made a fortune with this blanket. And that he donated it to homeless shelters and children's hospitals? What a lovely thing to give a child who may be frightened, alone, or awaiting a scary surgery. The person who had invented this blanket possessed the largest heart.

Yet he dared not take a hug for himself.

"So curious."

She folded the blanket and replaced it on the sofa. At that moment, her phone buzzed. She'd forgotten to place it back in the Faraday box after texting her mom. It was a text from her agent.

Shall I accept the offer? The publisher is waiting!

Pressing the edge of the phone to her lips, Saralyn closed her eyes. She could use that money as she settled into a new life. And so what if she delayed writing her Great American Novel for another five or six months while she ghostwrote the other story?

Thing was, she'd been delaying her move to self-reliance for over a year. Using the divorce as a crutch to mope and feel sorry for herself. The historical-heist story had been on the back burner for years. Of course, ghostwriting another story was the responsible choice to take care of her financial concerns. But it no longer felt right. How could she ever step into her new skin if she continued to hide behind the pages of another author's name?

Turning off the phone without answering the text, she placed it in the box and grabbed her sun hat. When in doubt, go sit on the beach.

A text from his CEO paraphrased what the social media had been buzzing about him the past few days.

Did David Crown quit this world? Where is he? The reckless billionaire is rumored to have fled for his private island. Was he more guilty than the innocent verdict declared?

He tossed his phone aside and it landed on his wallet where he'd pulled out the photograph. He looked at it every day. The boy's face smiled at him. Why did the media have to brew everything into a crazy maelstrom of lies? The facts regarding the lawsuit were clear. The trial transcripts had been released to the press. And he had not *fled*. He'd simply been done. Done with it all.

But they wouldn't let it go. How long did he have to stay hidden away on an island before the media circus moved on to the next sensational human, emotional wreckage?

He stabbed the machete he'd picked up for a morning of coconut hunting point first into the wooden countertop. The handle wobbled from the intense energy he'd released into it. Squeezing his hands aside his temples, he pushed his fingers through his hair and growled. He'd been so close to touching some kind of peace.

Yet he knew that while the island atmosphere relaxed and put him in a new mindset, it wasn't a cure-all. He needed to talk to someone. To put his feelings out there. Have them examined and recycled back to him in a manner he could sort through them all. It had been ages since he'd talked to a therapist. He'd gone his teen years and it had helped him to not necessarily forgive his parents for their lackadaisical and dismissive behavior toward him but rather to understand it. They had been raised as he had—at a distance and with nannies. They knew no other way to parent their own child.

That hadn't relieved him of the trauma they had unknowingly embedded in him since childhood. Yet he wasn't one to play the victim by clinging to the traumatic label and insisting he be treated with delicacy. He was a grown man. He owned his actions, and while he knew some actions were inadvertently the direct reflection of his younger years, he made a concerted effort to consider new ways to approach any issue that should arise. It was the inventor in him that allowed him to utilize creativity in most aspects of his life.

David loved his parents. Always would. But he would never make excuses for their distant parenting skills.

As for others in his life? Friends were few. David had quickly learned that the more money a man tallied in his bank account the more people wanted to cling to him, befriend him, share his air. All for the wrong reasons. He'd not gained a new friend he could trust since he'd invented the blanket. A few good buddies at the company that he could have drinks with and discuss women. Every man needed those. And the last time he'd seen Shaun, his best friend from high school, Shaun had been talking about joining the army and traveling the world. He'd looked him up online and had tracked him to Bangladesh. Shaun was currently stationed there with his wife and three children.

One day, David intended to visit Shaun. He

craved a reunion with someone who understood him. They'd met in Central Park one summer afternoon and had bonded over David's drone. Shaun had helped to fix a faulty wire in the remote and David had invited him over. Raised in a middle-class family, Shaun hadn't been impressed by the penthouse of pink marble and Gucci everything, but he had been curious over David's entertainment room slash laboratory. Together, they'd spent days sketching ideas for fantastical devices, shared quotes from favorite movies, and had learned each enjoyed reading about science and natural history. Shaun, being particularly tuned-in to David's emotions, had been the one to suggest David make a blanket that could give him what he'd not gotten from his parents—a hug.

David had been so busy he hadn't texted him in months. He should do that. Right now. Because if he let it slide, he'd only slip deeper into the void.

Insulated, was how he felt at times. A man alone in a world that rushed busily around him, pointing and staring and marveling and accusing, but never crossing the line to real communication and trust.

Something about talking to Saralyn made him realize she toed that line into his emotional needs. Probably she'd even smudged part of it away, for he'd told her some things about himself he never shared with anyone. He felt safe talking to her. Like a normal person who wasn't measured by dollar signs or even charitable acts. He could be himself with her.

But was she herself? Was he getting into something with a woman who might pull on a new costume and completely change? That seemed to be her goal. He liked the Saralyn he knew right now. She was beautiful, smart and daring. Sensitive and kind. She liked to laugh and be quiet. He had seen into the pain that she thought she could hide and wanted to erase, but it didn't frighten him. He understood it in ways he wasn't able to vocalize. She grounded him.

Aren't girlfriends there to ground and distract you?

Huffing out a breath, he shook his head at his deep wonderings. The woman had gotten inside him. And there was nothing at all wrong with that.

Picking up his phone, he calculated the time difference between here and Bangladesh.

A knock on the door brought a grin to his face. He called for Saralyn to come in and pulled on the shirt he'd tucked in his back pocket.

"Oh, don't do that," she said as she bounced in. The brightly colored bikini was back, which he appreciated. It enhanced her curves and drew his eyes to her bouncy breasts. Her smile beamed. "I rather like the view. You don't want all your hard work obtaining those muscles to go unappreciated, do you?"

With a smirk, he dropped the shirt. Just swim trunks? His usual island attire. And her lingering gaze did not make him feel demeaned. Hell, her attention felt great. As did the way she'd touched him last night. She had explored his skin with delicate fingers that had quickly become confident and brave. What a perfect kiss. The make-out session had ended too soon, but he could respect her need to take things slowly. They both had their emotional boundaries.

He quickly tucked the photo away in his wallet before approaching her.

"What's up with you this morning?" he asked. "You're more sunny than usual. Did something go well with your plotting?"

"I suppose you could say that. But it's nothing to do with my writing. My inner mermaid has plotted to come and steal you away and carry you to the depths. You up for a swim?"

He winced. "You didn't make that sound very appealing. I'm not much for drowning."

She laughed. "Sorry. I would never tuck away a man in a coral reef. We both know we're not up for the fallout following murder."

He laughed at that. No stomach for murder their shared trait? Ha!

"I am in the mood for a race," she said. "Breaststroke used to be my best event in high school. What about you?"

"Same. A race, eh?"

She nodded.

"Winner takes all?"

"Absolutely."

That she hadn't asked what *all* implied left it open for so many asks after he won. David set aside his phone and followed her out to the beach, which quickly turned into a laughing dash for the water.

After a triumphant, yet leery win, Saralyn waded to the big flat rock shaded by a curvy palm tree and sat. David followed. She had won by two body lengths. But as elated as she felt, she suspected the guy with more muscles than she'd ever own had let her win. And that annoyed her.

"Congratulations." David leaned in to kiss her.

She tilted away from his wet splashes as he sat beside her. Her prerace giddiness had fled, to be replaced by exhausted huffs. And a muscle-deep understanding that fifty was definitely not thirty-five. "I can't accept that win."

"What? Why? You're an amazing swimmer, Saralyn. That was a close match."

"Oh, come on, you let me win. I don't need any man to condescend to me."

"I didn't— Seriously?"

"Please, David, you've more muscles in one arm than I do in my entire body. Not to mention zero body fat. You could have easily overtaken me and won by a mile."

He lay back on the rock and blew out a breath. "It's been a while since I've used the breaststroke. I'm rusty! But believe what you want. Either way, winner takes all. You get to name your prize."

"I don't want a prize." It would feel like a participation trophy. Everyone got one, no matter the talent. Oh, but her muscles would be sore tonight. Fool! That's what she got for pretending she still had it.

Saralyn stood and stepped off the rock. "I'm going to shower and read this afternoon."

"You have to name a prize. It's only fair, Saralyn," he called after her.

Fair? Not really. But as exasperated as she felt by his claims to being out of practice—and she knew it was a lack of exercise that was making her testy—she shouldn't be such a party pooper. And that reminded her that a party lingered in her immediate future.

She stopped walking and wondered what a good ask would be. Something he might be able to acquire—and if he did, that would prove something to the hapless heroine. And make up for the race he threw.

"I want a cake," she called back. "For my birthday in a couple days. And not standard chocolate. It's gotta be unique. Fabulous! Worthy of fifty freakin' years."

"I accept the challenge, fair lady!"

A glance over her shoulder saw he'd turned to his stomach and rested his chin on his fist. Like a sunbathing merman with the occasional tendency toward knight-in-shining-armor. Those biceps could have won that race. And yet, he was more a gentleman than she perhaps knew how to relate to.

And she wanted to walk away from him?

Yes. She needed to brush off this icky feeling that he wasn't being honest with her about the win. Because it was her issue, not his. A dishonest man keeping secrets from her? Ugh!

Hoping he would get the hint she wanted to be alone, she wandered toward the villa. Regret tightened her mouth. She had been too quick with him. Too rude.

Why did a silly race bother her so much?

She wandered into the villa and veered into the bathroom, stripping off her swimsuit and hanging it on the rack to dry. Once under the warm shower stream, she pressed her palms to the glass-tiled wall.

She shouldn't have walked away from him like that. Her gut knew she could trust David. It was her heart, which had been ignored and bruised by her ex-husband, that had charged in and made a scene out there on the big flat rock. She didn't want to haul her baggage from a failed marriage into whatever was going on with David. He didn't need that. The man had enough emotional baggage himself.

Had she thrown up that wall to stall her blind stumble into a new life? That groove she knew she needed, but really, she was comfortable with her status quo?

"No, you're not comfortable," she muttered. "And, yes, you are stalling."

If she were going to move forward and find a solid position in this world, then she couldn't allow any preconceived emotions about romance to tarnish what she and David were creating. Because they were making something here on this beautiful island away from the world. And it felt too special to ruin.

If only for another week.

Twisting off the shower stream, she hastily dried off and squeezed the water from her hair. Dashing into the bedroom, she grabbed a floaty cream-linen sundress and pulled it over her still-moist skin. She couldn't be worried about what she looked like. There was a man out there who'd been hurt by her idiotic need to throw up a protective wall. Time to knock out some bricks.

Running outside, she spied David walking across the beach and called to him. He didn't stop walking. Fair enough.

She had just sort of won a hundred-yard breaststroke, and she was feeling every one of her fifty years, that was certain. Huffing up behind him, she called, "I'm sorry!"

He stopped immediately and turned to her. No smile on his face, but his expression did lighten as he took in her appearance. Saralyn tugged at her skirt hem, which she only now realized stuck to her wet thigh. She pushed a hank of hair from her face.

"I was reacting," she said. "I know you are kind and wouldn't do anything to hurt me. And even if you did let me win, it doesn't matter. I shouldn't have been so quick with you. I don't want you to think poorly of me. Things from… my past just sneak in and… And that's not fair to you. Past stuff is my stuff, not yours. Oh, I don't know how to say this properly."

He walked up and without a word kissed her. A heady, urgent, take-no-prisoners kind of kiss. The kind only heroes utilized to claim the heroine. To make her understand that she would have no other man but him kiss her. Tilting onto her tiptoes to keep it, Saralyn slid her hands up his bare chest and clutched gently at his shoulders, and then more urgently. He lifted her by the thighs and with a jump she wrapped her legs around his hips. They didn't break the kiss. If she'd felt depleted of energy on the run across the beach, now David's skin electrified every part of her being, invigorating her. His breath danced with hers. Their mouths knew one another. Heartbeats thundered a passionate timpani.

"Thank you," he said, setting her gently to the ground. "I felt bad that you didn't believe me. Maybe I didn't push myself as hard as I could. But I get it. I know you're dealing with some things."

"I don't want to bring those things into what's going on here. This island was supposed to be my safe space."

"Maybe you don't want me around? Would that make it easier to sit with your feelings and resolve them?"

"No." But what a generous and thoughtful offer. This island was also his safe space. And she wanted to respect that. "I don't want that weirdness between us. Can we…?"

She pressed a hand to his chest, measuring his pounding heartbeats against her palm.

Just be honest. Don't push away another man.

"I want you to kiss me again. And again. And then again. And after that…"

"Again?"

She plunged against his body and showed him exactly what she desired. One kiss. Then another. Until kisses become long streams of silent poetry shared between them, set to a cadence they created. It was giddying. So much so that Saralyn allowed the happiness that bubbled in her being to burst out in laughter. David joined her and they bumped shoulders and turned to walk.

They strolled along the shore. "I'm so glad you landed on my island," he said. "And that you chose the executive package and not the three-hour tour. We may have missed one another had you done so."

"The three-hour tour?" It had been a line in the theme song to the *Gilligan's Island* show; the castaways had only intended to be out for a few hours. "You seriously offer that?"

"Of course! It's sort of a joke, but some have taken it up. It's an afternoon of island fun and games. But don't worry, Mary Ann isn't expected to whip up any coconut cream pies."

"Coming from a former Mary Ann who is attempting to find herself, I thank you."

"You're far from Mary Ann. You are Saralyn. You are the universe."

"When you say that, it jars me out of every stupid judgment I've ever had about my body or my actions."

"Aren't we all the universe?" He nudged against her shoulder as they strolled, the warm sand sifting over their toes. "We're made of stardust and atoms and are electrical beings."

"Yes, and we're supposed to all be connected on a greater level. It's cool to think about."

"So, Miss Stardust, next time you feel lesser or affronted by a person or memories from the past, you need to remember how exquisite you are."

"Why is it so easy for you to be like this? So accepting. I thought you were here to escape your own troubles?"

"I am. But focusing on you slams the door on any troubles."

"Then you might never face them."

"I will. In my own time."

"Wise words coming from someone so young. I never would have thought I'd find myself attracted to a younger man."

He laughed. "You have a hang-up about the age thing."

"It's not so much a hang-up as…" What *was* it? He wasn't a floundering youth who couldn't relate to her on an emotional level. Nor was he an overzealous Lothario who only craved what he could get from her sexually. David was smart, self-made and had found his place in the world.

"The age thing is a dying cultural taboo," he provided, and when she began to protest, he rushed to add, "Hear me out. It used to be a shock to see couples of greatly differing ages. Now? Not so much. It's a generational thing. I don't see age when I'm dating. I see the person. You. What does it matter about age?"

"Well." What *did* it matter? A lot. At least, according to her *generation*, as he'd put it. And cultural influence. "As I've mentioned, it's my Hollywood conditioning. The way the industry treats women is reprehensible. Expecting them to maintain flawless skin, sex appeal and acquiescence."

"And the men can get old, fat and rich."

"I think men age more gracefully."

"Depends on the man. Trust me, you don't look a day over thirty."

"I'll take that."

"No arguments? You really are stepping into yourself, Miss Stardust."

"I think I am."

"Just one question about the age issue," he said. "What is it about a younger man that puts you off?"

"A lack of life experience and wisdom, for one. Also, the younger generation seems to have a different perspective on respect and kindness. Some seem so…entitled. I honestly believe it's a social media thing. Younger generations are literally being raised by the screen. But you're not like that. You feel like my equal."

"That is an immense compliment." He kissed the top of her head.

They walked for a while, wandering in and out of the tide. Not hand in hand, as she preferred, but their shoulders brushed. It reminded Saralyn of a photo her mom kept in her wallet of her dad and mom when they were dating. After a trip to Walt Disney World, they'd detoured to the Weeki Wachee Springs to see the mermaids, and that is where they'd gotten engaged.

Memories of her parents were precious and—they reminded her of a strange discovery her mother made.

"I have something odd to ask you," she said.

"Go for it."

To their left the horizon dashed purple below subtle orange and gold and pink. The waters had darkened, yet she felt safe walking alongside David. Her mother often told her that was how she felt whenever her dad took her hand.

"Walking here on the beach makes me think about my parents. They were so in love. My dad died ten years ago from brain cancer."

"I'm so sorry."

"Thank you. He went quickly. Sometimes death feels like a relief when you counter it with the suffering a person went through. Anyway, they were married for forty years. And just when you think you know a person left, right, up and down, you can discover something new about them. Even after death."

"Really? Your dad left a secret to be discovered after his death?"

"It wasn't left purposefully. After my dad died, my mom went through the old family albums that Grandma—my dad's mom—had given them when they were married. Mom intended to scan the photos and give them to Grandma on a CD. Mom got through half of them and noticed a photo that had been folded in half. It featured dad on the left and on the right was Grandpa. Both were sitting before a table, and it looked like Grandpa was looking at something.

"So she pulled it out and unfolded it, only to find whoever had folded the photo had done so to conceal the person sitting in the middle. It was a girl about my dad's age and she was showing her hand to Grandpa. On the back was a note that read *Showing Dad their engagement ring*. My dad had been engaged before he met my mom. But Mom had never known that. Dad hadn't said anything the entire forty years they were married."

"That's incredible. Was your mom upset?"

"Not really. It was just a weird thing to discover. But it made her realize that you can never completely know a person. So the reason I'm telling you this is, and it's a question I ask when I'm creating my characters, what is something about you that no one knows and might only learn after you're dead?"

"Ah? That's interesting." David shoved his fingers through his hair as he thought about it. She loved that unconscious motion. It flexed his abs and pecs and, his gorgeous dark hair glinted with a few water droplets. "Okay, I got it. But you can't tell anyone because then I'd have to kill you."

"You can't imagine how much I love that we both have murder-worthy secrets to share."

"Yes, well, if this got out, I'd be laughed out of the Normal Club."

"There is such a thing?"

"Apparently there is. Pretty sure they have badges and drive electric vehicles."

"And you think *you're* in that club? I'm not so sure about that. I rather think it would be a boring club. But do tell?"

"I was in a band once."

Saralyn spun before him, stopping their walk. She playfully gaped at him.

David offered a sheepish shrug. "It was a band that I formed with two friends, Shaun and Clive. We were fifteen. Practiced in Shaun's parents' garage."

"Seriously? That sounds cool. Not deathbed-secret stuff. What kind of songs did you sing?"

"Here's where the deathbed-secret stuff gets involved. It was emo scream metal. Called ourselves The Wretched Things. We were incredibly not cool."

Saralyn wasn't aware of that genre of music, but to imagine it put black clothing and long bangs on David with lots of silver studs and abrasive, gut-mined screaming. Not an image she would have ever conjured for him. "You're right. That one's a take-it-to-the-grave secret. Were you the singer?"

"Oh, no, I played…" With a grand splay of his hand, and a bow at the waist as if on stage, he announced, "Synthesizer."

Saralyn dropped her jaw open.

He nodded. "I know, right? You are swooning right now. I was very talented with the keyboard."

"I'm not sure if it's a swoon or…" Laughter sat just at the tip of her tongue. "I don't know that I've ever heard emo scream metal. And with synth? Isn't that an eighties band sort of instrument?"

"Totally."

"Oh, my God, you have to sing one of your songs for me."

"Definitely not. The synth player never sang. He just mouthed the words and flipped his hair."

David flipped back his hair dramatically. "I went to the salon and had it straightened. Wore the long bangs over my eyes. I embodied emo. All the girls swooned."

"I bet."

His laughter burst out. "Actually, we never played outside the garage. And I think we were together about three weeks. But I know there's a picture circulating somewhere. I'm sure Shaun has the original. One day, I will get it from him and burn it."

"Not if I find it first." She waggled her fingers before her. "My research skills are remarkably honed. If it's online, I can find it."

David clutched his chest in mock horror. "Would it dissuade you if I gave you my autograph?"

"Only a song will do. You must remember one of them?"

"I think we only had the one song. 'Cyber Chick.' Let's see…" He put out his hands and bent his fingers, then performed some piano-playing motions. *"Duh-dum-dee… Cyber Chick! You're so fine. Your bits and bytes turn me on."* More air-synth playing. *"Nah, nah, nah, nah, nah!"*

Bursting into a fit of giggles, Saralyn tucked her head against David's shoulder. "Oh, you win. I'm swooning!"

He flipped his hair and leaned in to kiss her. "We rock stars get all the girls."

"You can have me."

David made a show of setting his imaginary synthesizer aside and then tugged her close with a hand to her hip, his eyes never leaving hers. "I do want you, Saralyn."

She'd actually said that he could have her. Had she meant sexually or in a more general sense of her attention and devotion? Both sounded great.

"I have a plan," he suddenly announced with a glance to the sky, which was rapidly losing its golden hue. "Full moon tonight. Will you meet me for a swim up top?"

"Up top?"

"Haven't you hiked the tiny mountain yet? There's an infinity pool up there along with a badminton court."

"I haven't, but now I'm intrigued. A midnight swim?"

"No racing allowed."

"I'm in!"

CHAPTER NINE

AN INFINITY POOL overlooked the west side of the island and was a fifty-stair meander from ground level. Pristine hedges surrounded potted palm trees along one edge, and the water was as blue as the ocean. A poolside bar was fully stocked and of course David had poured wine before Saralyn had shown up.

This was the longest he'd stayed on the island. And he couldn't blame that entirely on the fact there were important matters in his life he needed to sort out. He could have done that in a few days, then hopped a flight back to New York. And it wasn't even because he felt as though he were being stalked by the press. Hell, he was. The daily calls from his COO confirmed that.

No, it was the fascination with Saralyn that kept him here. And she hadn't asked him to leave, so he felt lucky about that. He knew he'd have to face the issue he'd come here to resolve. And quickly. But not on this beautiful moonlit night.

"I can't believe how big the moon is." Saralyn rested her elbows on the edge of the pool, where if viewed from a distance, it appeared to spill over and into the ocean. "I think it's called a super-moon when it's so big and orange. And so close, like I could reach out and touch it. I wonder what my horoscope says about it."

"Do you follow horoscopes?" David rested the back of his head against the edge, his body floating out before him. From such a position, he couldn't see the moon behind him, but the soft glow on Saralyn's face mirrored its brightness. "What's your sign?"

"I am a Virgo. And yes, that means I like things done a certain way. Generally, I'm the only one who can do said thing the correct way it needs to be done. I'm methodical, but no, I'm not as frigid as we're made out to be."

"I've noticed your tendency toward warmth as opposed to cold." He cast her a wink. "I'm a Cancer."

"Birthday recently? I could have guessed that. You're very kind and put other people's feelings above your own. Sometimes to your detriment."

Nailed that one. It was always easier to let others do the emoting rather than himself.

"Happy belated birthday," she said, and tilted her wine goblet against his, which sat on a floating tray near them.

"Thank you. Thirty-five is an odd age. I'm not old but I'm not young. In the AI research-and-development world I'm considered an oldie, but in the finance-and-business-tech world I'm still a newbie. And we inventors can be any ol' age so long as we don't risk it by blowing ourselves up with our experiments. That's why I don't pay much attention to numbers. Who cares?"

"Sure, but you probably wouldn't date a seventy-year-old, would you?"

"Probably not. She'd be too wise to hang around someone like me."

"Are you saying I'm not wise? I like hanging around you. I don't feel as though we are so different age-wise. You get me. But you also don't make me feel like a matron. I'm your peer."

"You are my peer."

"Says the rock star with the emo bangs."

"You see? That sort of information gets out and I will never live it down. I trusted you."

"You still can trust me. I will never tell. And you know I'm a good secret keeper because I've ghostwritten more than twenty books and no one knows who they are for."

"Save the story filmed on this island."

She waggled an admonishing finger at him. "Just you, my partner in crime."

"Yes, yes. We have mutual blackmail material to hold over one another." He tilted back a double sip of wine and resumed a floating position. "You know I was thinking we never got to your confession regarding things one might only learn about you after you're dead. Give me something deep and dark that would surprise others."

She sighed and turned her head to rest against the pool edge alongside him, letting her body float and her arms sway out to the sides. David let his hand brush up against hers and she linked her pinkie finger with his. It wasn't quite holding hands. And it didn't make him uncomfortable. More of a means to anchor each other so they didn't drift away. A precursor to a real handhold? By all the desires he'd ever had, he hoped so.

"I'm not so sure I've ever touched deep and dark," she decided. "Hmm... Actually, it's something I think about a lot lately. Something that everyone expects from me. It's like they all know Saralyn will be fine because she does the being-alone thing so well."

David swept his body down and propped an arm along the pool edge. A moon goddess floated beside him. He could almost feel her heartbeats waver in the water around him. He wanted to touch her, to...hold her hand. To show some support, but... He wasn't sure it would be taken in the manner he hoped, so he kept his hand out, floating on the surface.

"After my death, people will be stunned to

learn that I actually never wanted to be alone," she finally said. "I've been there, done that. Surprisingly, I experienced it through a twenty-year marriage. I spent more time by myself than with my husband. Being a writer is a very insular thing. We writers don't drive off to an office to work and don't have office mates. We can't make friends over the watercooler. So, solitude is something I've grown into. Admittedly, I think I've done it well. But..."

A turn of her head searched his gaze. David swallowed. The conglomeration of stardust floating beside him radiated light, yet he could sense the darkness that shadowed that light.

"I'm afraid of being alone," she confessed. "It doesn't appeal to me anymore. I want the connection to people, to another person. I want a relationship."

"Like marriage?"

"I don't know about that. I became a virtual hermit in my marriage. No wonder he sought attention from other women."

"No, no, you're not going to blame yourself for Rock's indiscretions."

"Brock."

"Sorry. Rock. Brock. Stone. Granite. They're all a bunch of jerks."

"Hallelujah!" she cheered. Then she crimped

her brow. "I just know 'alone' is no longer interesting to me."

Pulling her closer to his body, David bowed
his forehead to hers. "You're safe with me, Saralyn. I would never do anything to hurt you."

"I know that."

"And you're not alone. You're with me."

Her hand slid down his neck and along his arm
under the water. "Let's stop talking about my ex
and focus on the romantic scenery. It's positively
bookworthy. It makes me want to kiss you."

He kissed her. "I can't stop touching you or
taking in your moon-kissed skin."

"Then don't."

After a heady yet splashy make-out session, they
moved to lie on one of the luxurious wide chaises
highlighted by the tumescent moon. They lay
side by side, not in a hug. It didn't bother Saralyn. Okay, it bothered her a little. She loved to
snuggle. She was actually snuggle-starved if
she thought about the rare times she'd managed to wrangle her former husband into a moment of quiet caresses. But she wasn't going to
press David for a need she had to accept he may
never be comfortable fulfilling. And really, if
she wasn't ready for sex, she mustn't test those
boundaries and give him the wrong signals by
suggesting they snuggle. That he'd stopped kiss-

ing her when she'd asked meant the world. This man was clued in to her emotional needs.

A surprising chill shivered over her skin as the palm fronds ruffled in the breeze. "Can you grab me a towel?" she asked.

He jumped up and retrieved one of the thick bamboo-colored towels from an open cupboard. Saralyn stood and wrapped it around her. She then kissed him, lingering at the corner of his mouth with a nip and a tease of tongue. His passionate growl did crazy things to her libido. And obliterated her nerves about making love. Toss the man down and have her way with him? The fantasy fit her mood. When she shivered, he rubbed his palms over her shoulders.

"Let's head back to the villa."

They strolled down the wide wood-and-tile steps. David's hair was drying slowly and his body gleamed in the moonlight. When she wanted to hold his hand, she remembered his aversion to doing that. As snuggle-starved as she, then. Neither of them really knew how to initiate what they both desperately wanted. Yet, weirdly, he had no qualms holding her close when they made out.

Was it that he needed the distraction of kissing to get him out of whatever mental trap his brain got caught in when approached by a hug? She was no psychologist. But she wouldn't let it rest. Now that the man had broken down her reluctance, she wanted to forge ahead and enjoy this slightly taboo affair with the sexy young billionaire.

Whew! A lot of new adventures for one day. And she didn't regret any of them.

CHAPTER TEN

LAST NIGHT, they'd fallen asleep on the couch after David had filled her head with all his fabulous and fascinating inventions in the works. They'd woke this morning, ate some fresh fruit, gone for a swim, and now he'd challenged her to a game.

"It's very odd that you have a badminton court in the center of the island." Saralyn selected a racket from the cabinet at court's edge. The infinity pool was on the other side of the changing rooms slash lounge lanai. "As opposed to the standard tennis court, I guess."

"Badminton is my jam." He tossed the white plastic bird into the air and caught it smartly. "Of course I'd put a court on my island. It was a no-brainer."

"Hand me that bird, Brainless. I get to serve first."

He clasped the bird to his chest. "What did you call this?"

She shrugged. "It's a bird or something, isn't it?"

"I am offended. You, the queen of research, don't know what *this* is called?"

"I've never played badminton. Only tennis. What is it?"

"Some call it a birdie, but the official name of this little projectile is a shuttlecock."

"A…" Saralyn covered a laugh with the back of her hand. Then she made an obvious glance down to his khaki shorts.

"Are you serious?" He waggled the plastic object before his face. "My shuttlecock is up here, you dirty-minded woman."

She swiped it from his hand. "My serve."

"You win again," Saralyn announced but not with any sign of disappointment. "As a man of your unparalleled talent should. But give me a few more years of practice and I'll give you a good challenge."

"I eagerly await the match."

David saw she put her arms up, moving in for a hug, and while his mind wanted to turn into her and boldly receive what she was offering, his body flinched and he moved against her with the side of his body, allowing her to wrap her arms across his back and chest for a weird embrace. The only kind he could manage without having a mental argument over the mechanics and emotional fortitude that was required of such an act.

Much as he knew it must be awkward for her, it was ten times more awkward for him.

Yet also, meaningful. Her actions spoke volumes to him. The hug was received mentally far more deeply than any physical action.

She pulled back and twirled her racket. "You're not much for hugs, are you?"

"Woman, I can kiss you silent and make your body sing with a mere touch. Why so worried about a hug?"

"I'm not worried." Though her side-eye glance did judge a little. "It just seems like you pull away whenever I try to hug you. Side hugs are not real hugs. Honestly, it's kind of weird for a guy who invented a blanket that literally hugs a person."

"I believe I told you I'm not much for hugs." A lie. He just wasn't skilled at giving or receiving hugs. Because he'd never had the experience to learn how they really worked.

"I don't get that."

Her persistence could not be ignored. He'd love to pull Saralyn into a big hug. Hell, he'd love to make love with her. They were getting closer to that intimacy. He was all about taking his time with her. However, she had but a week left and if he didn't act soon he may never win her trust. It's what he desired from her along with sexual intimacy. So that meant he had to be honest with her.

"Hugs are…the ultimate intimacy," he said. "More so even than sex."

Saralyn set down the racket and leaned against the supply cabinet. She wore a flirty silk skirt over her bikini and her movement set the ruffles into a sensual flutter. "Really? Because sex and making love both seem pretty darn intimate."

"You differentiate?"

"Of course. Making love is emotional and heartfelt. Sex is not. I mean, sex is great, and it can involve emotion. Eh, it's the romance writer in me. Don't think about it too much."

"I do think about making love," he said, "with you."

That arching eyebrow of hers always alluded to something she was willing to consider. Perhaps work into the new groove of a life she was shaping.

"Same," she offered confidently. "But first, give me the details on you and hugs. Or is it another death surprise?"

That made him laugh. Not nearly so surprising as him having formed an emo band when he was a teenager. But it was deep. And emotional. And… To spill a part of him that really didn't require spilling? Or rather, no one needed to hear about his awkward family dynamic.

And yet, he wanted to give Saralyn a part of him because he trusted her.

He took the racket from her and hung it with the rest of the equipment at the edge of the court. "Let's walk."

The wooden path spiraled down from the court to the mainland. A stroll was the de rigueur pace for any destination on the island. One of the parrots swooped over their heads but not low enough to make him thrust up a protective arm to protect Saralyn. They weren't eating. They were safe.

About halfway down, David stopped and gestured they sit on the massive tree step that had been carved in situ to create a portion of the stairway. It was now or never.

"Okay, here's the deal about me and hugs," he stated. "I was never hugged as a kid."

She tilted a startled glance at him.

He scrubbed the back of his neck, then offered, "The Crown family is not close or demonstrative. No hugs or kisses. Not even a vocal validation or approval of a job well done. Remarkably, I didn't realize until I was around nine or ten how little my parents touched me."

"Oh, David, I'm so sorry."

"It's what I've known, so it wasn't something I thought about much."

For the most part. But naming one's garage band The Wretched Things?

"Mom and Dad were jetsetters, involved directly in the everyday operations of the Crown family foundation and charities. They were rarely around the penthouse."

"What did they do exactly? Or do they do? Do they still work?"

"Yes, but not in a standard nine-to-five job. I explained that my great-greats invested in the telegraphy cables that brought the telegram to the world. That's how we came to our wealth. Old money. Because of those wise investments, we've never had to work, but my parents are type As who need to. Or rather, be busy. Running foundations and charities *is* work."

"Sounds like the best kind."

"It is, in that it keeps them busy and their minds sharp. I know, they're not that old, but I want them to age gracefully, and if they can continue their work, that'll be the fountain of youth for them."

"You care about them."

"Of course I do," he said, but softened the last word so it didn't sound like he'd been as offended as that comment made him. He did love them. In his own way.

"I could have gone the same route as them," he continued, "assuming a position on the foundation board and delegating to others, but since childhood I've always been interested in science and how things work. I enjoy creating new things. And tearing things apart to see how they work. It excites me. And I quickly learned a good day's labor gave me a serotonin boost. I can't imagine not having a physical job to challenge my brain and body.

"Anyway, while my parents tended their lives, I was basically raised by nannies. A very cold nanny in particular. She was astute and to the point. She never rewarded good behavior, nor did she punish. She was…unemotional. I didn't have parents to demonstrate emotion to me."

"You said something about the chef and his wife teaching you so much?"

"Exactly. I do love the LeDouxes for their kindness and for allowing a lonely boy to peer into their lives to see what real love was."

"So, your parents… They didn't hug you?"

He exhaled. "When they were around? No. 'Mum and Dad are very busy, David. We love you.' And then they'd wave and rush out the door for another few weeks. I…did attempt a hug one time. I believe I was nine. Well, it's silly to recall."

Yet it had influenced him in ways that affected him even to the present.

Saralyn slid a hand along his upper arm and gave it a squeeze. "Tell me?"

"It was one day at school, and I'd seen the parents waiting to pick up my fellow classmates greet their child with a hug and a kiss. I always marveled over that ritual. The kid would run into their parent's arms. No kid ever walked away from a hug frowning. So one day I gave it a go. Mom had stopped to pick me up—a rarity, but she had a meeting with the school's headmistress—and I ran into her arms for the hug. She reacted with offense, pushing me away and fretting over her white clothing. 'You wretched thing,' she said. 'You've dirtied my skirt.'"

David swallowed at the memory. It lodged in his throat and stirred a sickly quaver in his body. He thought he'd gotten beyond the emotional let-down of that experience, so it always surprised him that memory could summon the feeling as if it were yesterday.

"The name of your band," she said softly.

Saralyn's hand slid down his arm, stopping at his wrist. In that moment, when his heart felt open and safe, he twisted up his hand and clasped hers with his. She gave his hand a squeeze. It worked to tighten his chest and loosen something behind his eyes.

He nodded. "Seemed appropriate for a metal band, eh?"

She tilted her head against his shoulder. The caress worked like the real hug he so desperately wanted. And with her hand in his? The moment was not so frightening as he thought it should be. Instead, it warmed his very soul.

"So you didn't know the physical intimacy you were missing until you started dating?"

"Exactly. And then, you know girls and guys. We want to get our hands all over one another. The first time a girl hugged me, I sort of flipped out. And then when I thought about it, I realized it could be nice. But it never happened again. I mean, teenagers don't spend a lot of time hugging, they get straight to the good stuff."

"I get that. But I believe hugs are also the good stuff."

"Probably." Though he hadn't an actual *experienced* example to prove it to himself.

"Anyway, that 'lacking intimacy' led to me obsessing about connection with other people. I could make conversation, be in groups, have friends, even have sex with a woman. But the intimacy of two bodies hugging, of being fully clothed and quiet, and simply sharing… That disturbed and excited me. I wanted the feeling, but it scared me. But I also *needed* that feeling. So the safest way to get it was to invent the blanket."

"I take it you've some technical skills that made that happen?"

"Yes, I spent six years in college. I've a master of science in artificial intelligence, a biotech science degree and also computer coding, and an associate in electrical engineering. Seems like a lot, but I breezed through my studies." He shrugged.

"Learning comes easy for me. Anyway, I tried a few psychology courses, to add some variety to my education, but that bored me. I like tinkering and tech. Though the psych stuff did influence me. Do you know when a person receives or gives a hug oxytocin is released? A hug that lasts twenty seconds can reduce stress, lower your blood pressure, even your heart rate. There are studies that prove it can also boost your immune system."

"It's good for depression, yes?"

"You bet. And if you're feeling tired, a hug will give you a lift. It's utterly amazing what that simple yet impossible act can do for a person. After I learned all that, I had to invent the blanket. It was a no-brainer."

"I tried the blanket the other day. It really is marvelous."

"Thanks to a nudge from my best friend, Shaun, who possesses an uncanny ability to read people's emotions, I set out to help others," he said. "I knew it could be a good thing for kids in hospitals, elders in senior homes, some who are on the spectrum, anyone who was alone or unable to make a connection naturally."

"But just now you used the word *impossible* to describe a hug. The inventor of the most amazing blanket has never experienced a real hug? David, that makes me so sad. Makes me want to hug you right now. But don't worry, I won't. I think it has to come naturally for you."

"Thank you for understanding that. I want, more than anything, to hug you, Saralyn. But you're right, it has to feel…"

"I would never push you away," she said softly.

He nodded, thankful for her understanding. Then he lifted their clasped hands. "And look what you've accomplished. We're holding hands."

"I wasn't going to call attention to it."

"Did you think I'd be freaked?"

"Maybe."

"I was, which is why I kept talking as a means to distract myself." He studied their hands. "This feels…like we are putting our trust into action. In some synesthetic sort of manner I can actually see the trust. Do you think I'm a nut?"

"Not at all. Emotional synesthesia sounds cool. Yet I have to wonder, if your parents were never around, who was it that showed you how to be such a kind and generous man?"

"Oh, that's an easy one. Marcel, our chef!"

"Of course!"

"I spent a lot of time in the kitchen watching him prep and cook. He'd let me help him. But the reason I kept going back, despite the cuts to my fingers and the ridiculous inability to properly peel a potato, was that he talked to me like a real person. He was interested in whatever I had to say. He would encourage me when I told him about my latest crazy invention. And as a teen, I observed the love between Marcel and his wife. It was kind, respectful and a little fiery."

"I'm so happy you had that example to learn from. I wish you could have experienced the comfort of a hug growing up. But that lack pushed you to invent something that has helped so many."

"Yes, well…" Another text from his COO this morning had suggested it was time for him to return to New York City to face the press. "I'm thinking of pulling the plug on the whole thing. The lawsuit put a black mark on it all."

He didn't want to discuss the lawsuit. That was rife with emotions that he'd come here to sort out. On his own. "Let's go make something to eat."

She nodded, seeming to sense his need not to expound. Bless her for that. He'd opened a part of himself for her today. And their clasped hands proved he could trust her. But the dive had been deep, and right now he needed to come up for air.

CHAPTER ELEVEN

THE NEXT MORNING, as David was sweeping out the chef's cottage, his phone buzzed. He'd sent a text to Shaun ten minutes earlier.

How's it going, Crown?

Always well. But I miss you, buddy. It's been too long.

Feel the same. You're the one with all the cash. Fly in and spend a week with me sometime!

Let me know when and I'll be there.

Awesome. I'll check with the wife and get back to you. So, you at work?

On the island. With a woman.

Nice.

It's different. I respect her. And I want her at the same time.

Ah. Well, then, that's love.

David stared at those last two words. That was crazy. A pulsing red heart popped up on the screen. Now Shaun was just yanking his chain.

Love? It hadn't occurred to him that something so profound could be forming between him and Saralyn. Nah. Couldn't be. Love didn't happen so fast, did it?

Rationally, he knew it was possible. He'd read as much in his psychology studies and when he was researching for the blanket. And Marcel had always told him how he and his wife had experienced love at first sight.

Crazy, he texted back.

Whatever. Love sneaks up on a guy. Gotta go. My kid has soccer practice. Will text my schedule in a few days. Good to connect, Crown!

Same.

David turned off the phone and crossed his arms, leaning against the counter. Love? No, it couldn't possibly be.

And yet.

He'd never felt this way with a woman. The

many women who had moved through his life had appealed to him on different levels, and he'd enjoyed their company, treating them well, taking them out, learning about their likes and dislikes, having sex with them.

Sex is different than making love.

That was true. All those relationships had ended because he hadn't felt them right, in a way he couldn't define. He hadn't felt an ineffable connection to the woman.

Like an atom clinging to stardust.

A broad grin grew. "Well, all right, then."

When checking her phone for texts from her mom, Saralyn saw that Juliane had called two hours earlier. She immediately returned the call and Juliane gave her the lowdown on her living conditions: sparse and cold but homey, with a bookshelf stocked with old mysteries and an amazing AI microscope that generated simulations geared toward her project. Her fellow biologists were all men save one other woman. The two women did not feel threatened; it felt like family. And the food: yuck.

"How's the island treating you?" Juliane asked. "Is it just like the movie?"

Fluffing out her hair that was almost dry after a morning shower, Saralyn plopped onto the curved couch under the constellation chandelier and ran a hand down her bare thigh. "Exactly the same. Blue sky. Blue water. Endless bliss. I've been living in a bikini. Eating gourmet meals. Swimming with the fishes. Spending far too much time sunbathing. And have learned the finer points of badminton."

"Sounds like a dream, but despite the nearly one-hundred-degree temperature difference in our locations, I still don't regret missing out. Wait. Badminton? Are you playing...by yourself?"

"No, I'm playing with the self-proclaimed badminton champion, David Crown."

"The *owner* of the island? What the— Why is he there? And what's going on that you two are engaging in extracurricular sports? And please tell me that *extracurricular* extends to the form of sport I have in mind."

Juliane did have a dirty mind. The woman was a wonder when it came to helping her brainstorm sex scenes.

"If kissing is extracurricular, then yes," Saralyn said. "David is here because apparently the fine print allows him to stay anytime, even if there are guests."

"The fine print? Who reads that?"

"Right? But no worries. We've gotten to know one another and..."

"And...?"

Saralyn's sigh settled her deeper into the sofa

and the hug blanket flipped against her shoulder. She pressed it to her cheek. A truly kind person had invented this blanket. "I like him, Juliane. And the fifteen-year age difference doesn't bother me anymore."

"Ooh, Mrs. Robinson!"

"Oh, please, I am not some married older woman seducing a college student," she said, recalling the movie plot they both referred to. "David is not like any man I've ever known. He makes me believe that I can do this thing called *moving on.*"

"Saralyn, I'm so glad to hear that. But now I need the sordid details. Please tell me there are details that can be labeled sordid?"

With a laugh, Saralyn filled her in on their kisses and growing intimacy. And how he made her feel seen and not at all worried that anything he did see might offend him.

"He's been a balm for my soul," she said.

"You don't need balm, Saralyn, you need straight-up sex. I know it's been a long time since you've been with anyone but The One We Will Not Name, but you are a mighty woman who has survived a nasty divorce. Now it's your turn to take what you want."

"Me thinks you simply want to live vicariously through my sexual antics."

"Well yeah! What do you think I'll be doing

for the next six months up here with only a cell phone to talk to my boyfriend?"

They laughed and chatted about how one manages a twenty-yard walk outside in weather that hits minus double digits and if it might be possible to package up some tropical sunshine and ship it north.

When a soft tune started playing outside on the veranda, Saralyn smiled to recognize it as a romantic Sinatra song. She spied David standing in the open doorway, shoulder casually propped against the door, and a bouquet of those smelly purple flowers in hand. He made show of sniffing it, wrinkled up a disgusted face, then tossed them over his shoulder.

"I have to go, Juliane. Something sordid just walked in."

With a hoot and a clap, Juliane sent her "love" and "good luck," even as Saralyn turned off the phone and tucked it away.

Still propped in the doorway, David winked at her. "My plans to seduce you with flowers have failed. I forgot how stinky they are."

She strolled up to him and pretended to look around him to the scatter of purple and white flowers on the veranda deck. She could smell them even at this distance. With a crook of her finger, she gestured he follow her inside. "Your plans may not be entirely lost."

With that, she turned and he caught her by the arms as he kissed her soundly.

"I've been thinking of you since I woke," he said. "Probably even in my dreams."

"Lucid dreaming is what I do well. It helps me to plot my stories."

"How's our story going so far?"

"The hero has unknowingly slain a few minor dragons that have annoyed the heroine over the years."

"Really?"

She nodded. "Kiss me again. And then…"

"And then?"

She turned and strolled toward the bedroom, untying the silk scarf from her hips as she did so. Glancing over her shoulder, she revealed her best Mrs. Robinson–flirtatious eyelash flutter. And then she blew him a kiss.

David caught the kiss and pressed his fingertips to his mouth. As he approached, she leaned against the doorframe. He took her hand and kissed the back of it.

"No plans to hike the island this morning?" he asked.

She shook her head. "The wind is starting to pick up. And you know how I dislike the wind."

"I do know that. You like to stay inside."

"And be protected by a big, strong, handsome man." She couldn't even wince inwardly at that one. Nothing was going to change her mind. Every inch of her skin wanted David's attention, his touch, his kisses. And it was time she listened to her body instead of her erratic writer's brain.

"I'm strong," he offered.

"And handsome." She tipped onto her toes and kissed him. "I want to make love?"

He smiled against her mouth, then met her gaze. "Was that a statement or a question?"

No place for nervous jitters now. Saralyn Hayes was in her groove.

She tugged him inside the bedroom by the waistband of his swim trunks. "A statement."

He closed the door behind him and pulled her into his arms as they tumbled onto the bed.

Saralyn lay in bed beside David. They'd made love. For hours. An orgasm here. A wander into the kitchen for refreshment. Luxuriously slow kisses and delicious touches. Another orgasm. Light chatter about their favorite positions and then performing them.

Now they lingered. The wind had softened and fluttered the curtain and a symphony of bird-song danced through the open window. David had drifted to sleep. A light afternoon nap. He deserved it after his vigorous performance. All afternoon. And she'd kept up with him. Her sexual stamina had not suffered because of divorce, aging or menopause. It was refreshing to know that. No old lady here!

Lying on her side, her hand resting on David's chest, she replayed their conversation about his inability to accept a hug. Not for lack of trying. What a cruel mother to have pushed him away like that. The distant parenting. It had obviously shaped him in ways both good and bad. The good was the invention of the blanket that helped so many. The bad, well. She just wanted to pull him into a hug and show him how much she cared. But she didn't want to frighten him.

It was odd that he was so comfortable with her in bed, sharing his body, licking over hers and lying against her, skin against skin. But it wasn't a hug. When they made love, they moved against one another, laughed, kissed and touched. Yet it wasn't a moment for quiet, listening to one another's heartbeats or simply hugging.

Snuggling beside his warm body, she stroked her fingers through his soft, dark chest hairs. He smelled like the sea, the foliage and earth, and her body coiled instinctively toward his strength. Safe here with him.

Could it last? Did she want it to last?

While the idea of making love to a man and then *not* starting a relationship seemed to be the norm in today's society, if she were honest with herself, she still clung to her ingrained beliefs.

This intimate connection meant something to her. She never would have invited him into the bedroom if it hadn't. She didn't want it to be surface or discarded as a hookup. And she did not care to be alone anymore. Been there, done that throughout her twenty-year marriage. Creating a deep and lasting connection with a man was important to her.

Was David the man who could connect with her as she navigated her way through this new chapter of her life? Was she jumping in too quickly?

She shouldn't think too far into this. Just enjoy the moments. It wasn't as though she had many days left on the island…

She'd come here to make some life decisions, not gain a lover or boyfriend. Once she set foot off this island, she had much to take care of. Moving. Writing. To ghostwrite or not? She still hadn't decided! And when calling Juliane, she'd seen another text from her agent.

It would be easiest to take the ghostwriting job. How long could she put off taking that big and scary step into independence?

"I will make a decision. Before I leave the island."

But for now, and perhaps the rest of the day, she intended to luxuriate in David Crown.

And so she did.

CHAPTER TWELVE

TODAY WAS HER fiftieth birthday.

And she was on a gorgeous tropical island and had acquired a younger lover. What a way to walk into that auspicious age!

A tango echoed softly from the speakers set at various places around the island. Saralyn could generally locate the area where the sound was coming from, but she'd yet to spy an actual speaker. Likely they were in the shape of a coconut. This song she recognized from one of her favorite movies about married assassins discovering they had been assigned to take the other out.

After rising this morning and making silly love in the shower, they'd shared a quick breakfast. But the insistent pings on David's phone could not be ignored. Apologizing, and insisting he keep all business away from the bliss they had begun to create, David had gone to the chef's cottage to make a few phone calls. She'd sensed the tension in his tone as he'd kissed her quickly and then wandered off. What he'd come here to escape had followed him. She certainly hoped he was able to overcome it.

She'd taken to picking flowers. These blooms smelled like candy and had interesting long stamens. Tiny birds flocked to them, sipping from deep within. She didn't pick many; it felt wrong to spoil the scenery and they were so big. Three vibrant pink blooms, each as big as a cat's head, would fill the villa with a heady scent.

The world felt lush and sensual. Her eyes viewed it anew without the tedious doldrums and disappointments of decades past. Had good sex done that? Yes!

Turning dramatically, she clutched the thick flower stems and performed a makeshift step to the music. She had no clue how to tango. Didn't matter. She felt free and unencumbered. Today was her birthday. And she intended to celebrate every molecule of it.

She hadn't mentioned the auspicious day to David over breakfast. If he remembered, great. If not, it didn't matter, because who really needed to be reminded by a handsome younger man that she was older?

Stop it, Saralyn!

She wasn't thinking like that anymore. Age meant nothing to David. And she was beginning to respect his point of view on that subject.

She didn't have to subscribe to any preconceived expectations!

Shaking her hair to feel it dust her shoulders, she spun and performed a few steps across the sand. Swaying her hips, she surrendered to the sensual pull. When someone clapped from behind her, she spun and smiled through the bouquet. The urge to drop her shoulders, bow her head and make herself a ghost did not arise.

No longer would she stand behind a man.

Lifting her arms and infusing the air with the floral fragrance, she swiveled her hips and went off script with the tango and into her own sensual dance. It felt good to move her body to the rhythm of the nearby waves.

When she turned, David had squatted and rested his chin in hand, his attention completely on her. The hero enraptured? Silly romance. What mattered to her was that she felt safe to dance before him. And a little naughty.

With a wave of her hand and a shift of her hips, she embodied the music. Closing her eyes, she concentrated on the air that brushed her skin and sifted through her hair. Intoxicating fragrance spilled over her being. The regard of her lover as she danced before him felt tangible, soul deep.

No, she wasn't dancing for him. She danced for herself. For the woman she was determined to embrace, respect and honor. Saralyn Hayes was fifty years old, had a beautiful life, and could make any decision she wished to make. From this moment forward, it was all good.

"You seduce me with your confidence," he said.

"I think I've seduced myself." She dipped and handed him the flowers, then spun out into a fun twist and hip shimmy. "I've never danced for myself before!"

"Your beauty puts these flowers to shame."

She was about to counter that compliment when her heart rushed in and stopped her. *Just accept it!* So she did.

"You can join me if you like."

"Nope. This dance is all yours, Miss Stardust."

"Sounds like a lounge singer who croons into one of those old-fashioned microphones." She grabbed an imaginary microphone and announced, "And singing at the Galaxy Lounge tonight…ladies and gentlemen, Miss Stardust!"

David whistled and clapped and leaned back to catch his elbows in the sand, the flowers abandoned near his side. "Bravo!"

Saralyn performed a final spin, feeling every ounce of joy and happiness explode out of her in laughter. Turning, she dove next to David and kissed him.

He brushed the hair from her cheek and kissed

her nose. "I hope that's not the last performance by Miss Stardust I get to watch."

"She only does private engagements. And I'm pretty sure only for men named David with the last name Crown."

"Eh, there could be quite of few of us in this world. I'm immediately jealous."

"I promise to reserve all seats only for those David Crowns who own tropical islands and who can spear a fish."

"I promise to show up for every performance. So what has compelled you to dance on the beach like a flower goddess summoning the sun?"

"The music tempted me, and all of a sudden, I…became myself."

"You inspire me, Saralyn. I hope someday I can dance by myself. Metaphorically, that is."

"You already do that. But I know something has sidelined you lately. Work stuff." And he didn't want to talk about it, so she would respect that. "But dancing with a partner is more fun." She climbed onto his lap, knees in the sand to either side of his hips and pushed her fingers through his oh-so-soft-and-curly hair, tilting his head up toward her. "You are one sexy man."

"Miss Stardust thinks I'm sexy? Nice." He rolled her to her back and the twosome made out on a fragrant crush of flowers.

But too quickly, Saralyn wriggled uncomfortably. "Sand in my bikini."

"Take it off."

"You think?" She glanced up and around.

"Don't worry, the professor and Mary Ann are on the other side of the island, and I know the rest of the gang are doing things on their own. We're alone."

"Yes, but the sand is moving into uncomfortable places. Let's take this inside, shall we?"

He stood and helped her up, grasping the crushed flowers as she did so. Displaying the pitiful bouquet, he pouted mockingly.

Saralyn grabbed the bouquet and took off running toward the villa. "Catch me if you can!"

They didn't make it to the bedroom. Once on the veranda, Saralyn turned and blew a kiss to David. He caught it and crushed it against his chest. And in a bold move, she slipped off her bikini top and tossed it at him.

They landed on the padded veranda sofa amid kisses, caresses and frenzied clothing removal. All the heroes she had ever designed for the page had stepped into her reality. But they didn't embody David Crown. He was his own man. Far above any fictional creation. He was real, genuine and felt like a piece of her she'd never known was missing until she touched it now.

They came together quickly, easily, sharing

themselves and moving like a well-choreographed tango that took and gave, and insisted and then surrendered. For the first time in her life, Saralyn landed in her orgasm freely and without reserve. She shouted and gripped her lover's hair and moved her body as tight to him as she could and then she let go and floated. In his arms.

He came as quickly and loudly, settling next to her on the sofa and huffing soft breaths filled with levity and joy. "That's so good."

"I agree," she said on an effusive gasp.

They lay there under a canopy of palm fronds, tropical flowers and birdsong, clasping hands. If this moment might never end, Saralyn would take it, no questions asked. She'd never felt…

"Are you happy?" she suddenly asked her lover.

"Right now? Hell, yes. You make me happy."

As was she. But. "I mean, overall. With your life." She turned onto her side and spread her fingers through his fine chest hairs, taking a moment to study his fast heartbeats. But her curiosity would not be curtailed. "If you put aside this escape to the island to get away from whatever is troubling you, can you say that your life is generally happy?"

"Kind of an intense question for having just made love. I'm still flying on that orgasm."

"I promise you'll get to fly again. But I do believe you are more adept at avoiding uncomfortable questions than I am."

"Fine. I'll play." He threaded his fingers through hers and kissed her hand. "Despite the stuff going on with Crown Corp? Yes, I'd say I'm generally happy."

"How do you know that?"

"Because… I've never wanted for anything materially. And I feel…well, not mad, bad or indifferent."

"A lack of harsh feelings does not make for happiness. What about wanting for something emotionally?"

"You can try to convince me I'm an emotional wreck all you like, Miss Stardust, but trust me, I am very aware that life has treated me well and I am grateful for that and have no real reason to be unhappy. What about you? Are *you* happy? Setting the divorce aside."

"I am. I'm content." She rested her chin on their hands, which he held on his chest. "Maybe too content. Especially when it comes to living like a ghost and avoiding interaction with people. I'm also not mad, bad or indifferent. I just think happiness is an inside job. Like a person shouldn't rely on anyone else for that feeling. You said I make you happy." For how long? Their time together was growing shorter! "But what about when I'm not around?"

"A person's mood can lift and improve and you don't need to label it as *needing* that other person, like some sort of happiness parasite."

"Now I'm picturing what such a parasite must look like, with tentacles and bright pink eyes."

He kissed her. "Save that for a science fiction novel. Life treats me well. Most of the time. And for that, I am happy."

Saralyn closed her eyes. "I'm going to start truly living in my happiness. Embodying it. To genuinely not rely on others for a good mood or even a ruined moment. I want to take responsibility for everything I say or do. I will create my own life."

"Seems like you're doing it."

"It does, doesn't it?"

"You dancing before me was like watching confidence. I know you've the past clinging to you, but each day, you shake off a little more. I don't think it will happen like a snap of the fingers."

"Shaking it off is a good way to put it. I'll probably dance it off." She twirled a finger in one of his dark curls. "I like what's happening here. Between the two of us. Beyond the sex."

"Same."

"When I leave the island, will it all reset and go back to the way it was before I set foot on these gorgeous warm beaches?"

"I don't want it to."

Neither did she. But she didn't live in New York, where she could be close to him. In a few months, she wouldn't even have a home. Was starting something with David worth the challenge? Would he be receptive to her wanting a man in her life? Even if she didn't live in his city? It was too much to bring up. It felt like she was forcing him to commit.

And they were both naked. Weird time to talk about the big issues.

"We'll see what happens, eh?" she offered lightly. "I'm going for a walk around the island." She kissed him and sat up, searching for her swimsuit pieces.

"You've stopped holding your stomach in," he commented as he watched her dress.

"I..." She sucked in her stomach, then released it. "What?"

"You've been doing it since the first day we met. A woman thing. I noticed you've become more relaxed. More yourself."

She smoothed a hand over her belly. He was right. She had relaxed. She'd not even given it a thought yesterday during their all-day sex session. This soft belly was all hers. Time to own it!

She pushed out her stomach in an exaggerated bulge. David laughed. And she laughed with him. Leaning over the sofa, she kissed him. "Catch you later."

"I've some business to take care of, but yes, I will find you later, Miss Stardust."

Following a post-sex snack attack of pepper-spiced hummus and veggies, David finished the phone calls he'd started before he'd been distracted by the dancing lounge singer on the beach. Much as he had separated himself from work, work always knew where to find him. There were questions to answer, contracts to approve and a marketing plan that required his notations on a pdf slideshow.

And the looming decision. Apparently reporters had started to camp outside Crown Corp. His COO had sounded nervous. He'd taken it upon himself to get public relations to look at their options regarding cooling the media's curiosity. David was confident the man could handle it, but he couldn't ignore the call to duty. To his very honor. He had to return to New York, and soon.

But not yet.

After speaking to the home office, he made one more important call. The delivery would take a few hours to arrive. As he set down the phone his thoughts drifted to the only other person on the island. What was he feeling about Sara-lyn, aka Miss Stardust of the Galaxy Lounge?

She had touched parts of his psyche he'd never thought available to others. He'd *held her hand*. That was an emotional connection on a completely different level than the amazing lovemaking they'd shared.

There was so much going on inside him emotionally, what with work and now this island experience, it was almost too much to sort out.

Yet his intention to get straight whether he should stop producing the hug blanket was set aside. He'd been too preoccupied with the wondrous feeling of being near Saralyn. She made him forget all the bad stuff. And he knew, rationally, that a person should never depend on anyone else for happiness. He had to feel happy before he could be with another person. But *did* he feel happy?

Yes, more than he had felt so in years. All his life? Possible.

Shaun's words returned to him. *Love sneaks up on a guy.*

He was falling for Saralyn. And that felt like something he wasn't allowed to have, such as a hug. He had to overcome that reluctance. Because if he could not, then he risked losing the best thing that had ever danced into his life.

CHAPTER THIRTEEN

As FAR AS fiftieth birthdays went, this one topped the charts. Saralyn was on a beautiful tropical island, currently floating in the azure waters like an abandoned blowup chaise. She had taken a lover. The most handsome, respectful, sexy, arousing man she knew. She had begun to embody herself, to really feel her bones and skin and enjoy simply being a woman. A person who deserved notice and respect! And she was *this close* to walking away from the ghostwriting offer. Everything felt right.

How to frame this moment and keep it forever?

Because soon enough, she'd have to return to reality. Leave behind David Crown and his sensual kisses and masterful lovemaking. Well, she didn't have to leave him behind. They could…

What *could* they do? Have a long-distance relationship? Saralyn wanted nothing to do with such an impossible arrangement. If she dated a man she wanted him close, in the same town. She didn't do sexting or the whole "distance makes the heart grow fonder."

It was all or nothing, baby.

Could she have it all from David?

All the attention. All his laughter. All his confident smiles and brazen stares. She wanted the wild and sensual sex with a younger man. The fiery shivers that his touches ignited throughout her being. The feeling of being so wanted, so desired, as if she were the only thing that mattered to him. She wanted to walk alongside him and notice when others glanced a bit too long.

What's that? She's so much older than him. And he's so young. Interesting.

Saralyn wanted that *interesting.* She wanted that attention. She wanted to be noticed!

Swishing her fingers to spin her body on the surface of the water, she closed her eyes and smiled to herself. If she and David took their affair off the island, she would be noticed. The man attracted the media's attention. Could she do that again with another man?

The real question was, could she stand *alongside* another man, holding his hand, and be his equal? As opposed to standing behind in the shadows, the supportive one, and being okay with that. The shadows had grown cold and uninviting. And when had Brock ever returned with support for her career?

Standing back and looking over her relationship with Brock now, it was much easier to see the manipulation on his part. Keeping her at home, writing and earning just enough to be satisfied but never to support herself. He had been a necessity, her provider. And she'd gotten stuck in that blind thinking.

And no, she wouldn't accept all the responsibility for her husband's wandering eye. She had tried. She had been there for him. That marriage, to that man, just hadn't been the right place for her. And she realized that now.

David felt like the right place. But would he want her by his side for all to see? This may very well be an island fling for him. Enjoy a few weeks together, then, "See ya later, Miss Stardust."

She had to ask him where his head was at with all this. She needed to know. And she would.

After she'd floated on this sunny tropical dream for a while longer.

At the sight of the motionless body floating near the dock, David dropped the two green coconuts he'd cut for an afternoon refreshment and burst into a run. It could only be Saralyn. And… she wasn't moving. Had she drowned? Her body floated to the surface?

His heart thundered. Every muscle tightened

and made breathing difficult. She was an excellent swimmer, but anything was possible.

He raced across the dock and jumped into the water, landing beside her body with a splash. Gripping her by the shoulders he lifted her, and at the same time, she sputtered and slapped the water's surface.

David swore and released her. Dark thoughts gripped him. Flashes of sitting in a courtroom. *Viewing those terrible photos.*

"Saralyn, I thought you were dead."

"What? David, don't be silly. I was floating. You look like you've seen a ghost."

"I thought I had." He swore again under his breath, heaving in air and wincing as his lungs protested his flight to rescue. She was fine. Yet he'd thought the worst. And had seen…such achingly horrendous images. And oh, but one tragedy had been enough of late. "I don't need another death in my life."

He straightened and squeezed his eyes shut, tilting back his head. Every part of the trial revisited his thoughts. The detailed report given by the coroner. The heart-wrenching confession of the mother and then the father. It had been too terrible. And when he'd thought Saralyn dead, his heart had raced to the same dark place that squeezed his chest so tightly he still gasped to breathe.

"I'm fine," she said too brightly from behind him. "Want to go for a swim?"

He shook his head and stalked toward the shore. "I can't do this right now."

"What? David, what's wrong?"

"Need to be alone," he muttered. "Sorry. Feelings…conflicted. I need to get this figured out."

When his feet hit dry sand, he took off in a jog.

The day hadn't ended exactly as Saralyn had wished. Since David had tried to rescue her from floating in the ocean, she hadn't seen him. And after hearing him mutter something about not needing any more death in his life, she'd sensed in that frantic moment he'd gone to a dark place. He'd said he needed to be alone. To figure things out. So she'd respected that and given him his distance.

But it was late. The golden waning moon hung low in the evening sky. She sat on the veranda, wearing the fluttery red sundress she'd packed specifically for today. It represented her bold step into the next chapter. The urge to perform some sort of ritual to take back her power and confirm her commitment to moving forward niggled. But what to do? The day had been a leisurely and pleasurable venture into self-care. This entire vacation had been so!

What she really wanted was to spend the last

few hours of her birthday with David. Dare she seek him out? She would apologize for giving him a fright. Maybe he'd talk about it with her. She wanted to see inside all those places he kept secret and closed. Because seriously? She wasn't the only one who had fled to this island to work things out. David wanted certain things as well. She had been too focused on herself to realize that until now. She must be more cognizant of his needs. And tonight that meant privacy.

Collecting two of the portable solar lanterns from the veranda—one in each hand, dangling at her sides—she walked out onto the beach, wandering for a while. Eventually she found herself at the big flat rock that provided the best seating for twilight sea-gazing. Placing a lantern to either side of her, she sat. Ribbons of pink and violet streaked the darkening sky. The air tasted salty and the musical chirps of tropical birds echoed out from the trees behind her.

Resting her elbows on the rock behind her, she stretched out her legs and could just splash her toes in the water. "Happy birthday to me."

It wasn't as though she hadn't spent many birthdays alone. Brock had tended to forget or to work late, or to grumble about getting a reservation at a trendy place at the last minute. After a few years, she'd given up on reminding him and had quickly learned to treat the day as any other day.

She had lessened herself so as not to outshine him. She knew that now. Never should she have completely extinguished her light.

"I will shine," she announced to the sky. And then whispered, "Like Miss Stardust."

Still. She felt…unsatisfied.

Growing older shouldn't have to be a buzzkill. In fact, it required creativity and engagement, even if she was all alone. She could make her own party. There was wine back at the villa…

Saralyn turned to see David walking toward her. He wore rumpled white linen pants and an unbuttoned white shirt that revealed his chest hair. In one hand, he held a wine bottle, and in the other, he balanced a plate on what looked like a computer tablet…

"Happy birthday!" He sat beside her. "Did you think I would forget?"

She had. A twinge teased at her eyes, threatening a tear, but she shook her head.

"I'm sorry about earlier," he said. "I shouldn't have yelled at you. Especially on your birthday."

"You didn't yell at me. And I feel sure you were panicked and not in the right place for the casual swim I'd suggested. You thought I had drowned. I didn't mean to give you such a shock."

He tilted his head against hers. "I'll explain.

But not tonight. Now is for the birthday girl. That dress is…wow."

His inability to describe how he felt hit her just right. She'd dumbstruck the hero? Go, Birthday Girl!

He set down the bottle and tablet and then displayed the plate, which held a small, elaborately decorated cake. White fondant embellished with lacy pink curls and coils blossomed into red and violet flowers. It looked like the island's tropical blooms had landed on the cake. And it sparkled!

"That's amazing. How did you…?"

"You did request a cake. And I do have connections."

"Marcel?"

"He was thrilled to go wild with the flavors, which he said would be a surprise. But I forgot candles."

"That's probably best. We don't want an inferno spoiling the goods."

He handed her the plate, which she lifted to her nose to smell. Sugar city!

"Don't dig in yet." He picked up the tablet. "Tonight, the Galaxy Lounge is featuring the former synth player from The Wretched Things." He tapped the tablet screen and musical notes sounded.

"Oh, this is going to be good!"

"Happy birthday…" he sang. Another run of

musical notes emulated a synthesizer. *"Happy birthday to you."* He performed a head-banging move and then flipped back his bangs to smile at her. *"I don't know the words, so I'll just end with the grand finale…"*

An exaggerated performance filled the air with an array of notes that sounded like "Happy Birthday" with an emo metal edge to it. And then with the last note, which he held down to extend the tone, he announced, "Thank you, everyone! We're here all week. Be sure to give the birthday girl a big round of applause!"

Lifting his fingers from the keyboard, he clapped, cheered and even tossed in a wolf whistle before bowing his forehead to hers and kissing her on the nose. "Happy birthday, Saralyn." He tugged a fork from a pocket in his shirt. "Dig in."

She took the fork and paused to absorb what had happened. The man had serenaded her, and he'd exposed a part of himself that he'd tucked away hoping to never experience again. She could fall in love with David Crown.

What was stopping her?

"You going to eat that or count the calories?" he asked with a nudge to her arm.

"Calories don't count on one's birthday." She stabbed the center of a bright violet flower and claimed a piece. It was indelicately large, but she shoved it in her mouth and closed her eyes. Oh, mercy. Not too sweet, and deliciously creamy frosting. Tangy fruity flavors burst on her tongue. Perhaps yuzu or some tart/sweet citrus. Heavenly. Rich.

Saralyn moaned. Now *this* was real love.

"That good?"

"Hold that plate still." She stabbed for another bite. "I haven't had cake this delicious maybe ever. Did you grow up being served cake like this? My goodness, it's so gooey yet dense. I… Turn the plate. I want to taste that red flower."

While he held the plate, she forked in a few more bites. Then she had the consideration to offer him a taste.

"About time." He opened his mouth and she fed him. "Yep, that's Marcel's four-star work, for sure. Another."

With a bite of cake in his mouth, he leaned in to kiss her. Sharing the mushy, cake-y kiss made her giggle. When he dashed out his tongue to lick her upper lip she returned with a nip to the corner of his mouth. They made a mess of one another, but it was the best birthday cake she'd had in fifty years.

"How does it feel to be fifty?" Swiping his mouth clean with the side of his hand, David reached for the wine bottle and took a swig.

"No different. And…very different, actually. I

feel lighter, if that's possible. Like I'm still floating. But also a little sad for the years behind me."

"Why is that?"

"I've been asking myself, were my married
years a waste?"

"No time is ever wasted if you can rescue the
good memories and learn from the bad."

"So philosophical."

"Eh. I think I read it on one of those inspira-
tional wall posters in an office once."

Saralyn laughed and swiped a finger across a
smear of frosting on the plate, which sat on her
lap. "I don't feel old."

"You're not old."

"I honestly believe, in your eyes, I'm not."

"Old is a state of mind. But. Probably around
eighty, a person can claim oldness. I mean, eight
decades should constitute wisdom and knowl-
edge and having the right to tell others what to
do."

He handed her the wine bottle. Before sipping,
she said, "I want to do this with you when we
leave the island."

She heard his inhale through his nose, but he
didn't reply.

So he didn't feel the same? Shoot, she'd guessed
wrong about him. This was just a fling for him.
"Or not. I mean, this is just a fling for you, so—"

The kiss wasn't meant to silence her but rather

silently ask for time, or so she suspected. And hoped. He wasn't yet ready to go there.

"I want you to have everything you desire," David said. "You're beautiful in the moonlight. I want to make love to you."

He'd cleverly avoided answering her inquiry about this being a fling. But as he leaned over her, his eyes delving into her soul and his body reading hers without even asking, she surrendered to his atomic pull on her stardust. They made love on the rock under the waning moon. With the occasional bite of cake to fortify and fuel them with more energy.

CHAPTER FOURTEEN

THE DAY FOLLOWING her fiftieth birthday felt like just another day. No cosmic awakening. No stunning transformation in her body. Not even minions bowing and asking to fulfill her every desire.

Really. Was it too much to ask for one tiny minion?

Waking this morning with inspiration gnawing at her brain, Saralyn had foregone the swim that David suggested. His non-response to her asking about this being a fling still cautioned her. Placed a narrow crevice between them that he seemed not to notice. Sending him off with a kiss, she showered and wrapped a robe about her body. Maybe she was overthinking things. Had to be.

Most certainly she was.

With a glass of fresh-squeezed guava juice and a plate of eggs beside her, she typed away on her laptop. Yes, she'd dug the laptop out from the Faraday box. The characters she'd created for her historical heist insisted she pay attention to their troubles instead of her own. And that was as good excuse as any to avoid the tough emotional questions. Right now the youngest thief was questioning her ability to pull off the heist of the century—stealing the famous Marie Antoinette necklace—while the other thief just wanted to get back home. To her own time.

How Saralyn did love a twist!

Fingers flying and her muse slinging words top speed, she glanced to her now-cold eggs and then looked back to the screen. The *shush* of waves not seventy feet from where she sat on the veranda couldn't entice her away from the story. Nor did the bird chatter fluttering overhead. Sunshine warmed her bare legs—writing in a bathrobe was decidedly freeing—and even the throat-clearing sound of the world's sexiest island hero couldn't compel her fingers to halt.

"Writing?" David asked the obvious that tended to make all writers roll their eyes.

Saralyn didn't bother with the roll. "Yep."

"Got it. Had my swim. Thinking about spearing some fish. I'll check in with you later."

"Yep."

"But I'm taking these." The plate beside her disappeared. "Cold. But not terrible."

She allowed herself a moment to pause and follow his retreat off the veranda and across the beach. His swim trunks couldn't hide that nice tight—

"No sex scenes in this story," she said, remembering, and placed her fingers back on the keyboard. "Only in real life."

With a burst of a smile, she resumed her work.

David had no desire to disturb Saralyn when her concentration looked absolutely riveted. He knew that feeling of chasing an idea or a muse. Some of his best days were spent alone in the lab deeply immersed in creation. Those were the days he only surfaced after dark with a smile and a bounce to his stride. Good times.

As he wandered the beach, eating the cold eggs with a fork, he marveled over how writers could create entire novels, conjuring complete worlds from their imagination. It seemed an impossible task. He did love a good mystery or thriller. But to possess such skill as to put it all together? Incredible. Of course, what he did was similar. He took an idea and brought it to fruition. Like his current project. The Body Tuner—based on the Solfeggio frequency to naturally heal—was a result of years of mental creation, followed by months of technical research and bringing it to reality. Every moment fueled by imagination and creativity.

Realizing he felt some sort of domestic peace

at having seen Saralyn work, casually stealing her breakfast and then wandering off, his steps lightened. The woman captivated him. Everything about her interested him. From her shy smiles that quickly switched to a self-assured lift of her chin. To the quiet moments when her brain went on an inner trip to another world, despite her standing firmly in reality.

What a fool her husband was to have looked to other women to satisfy himself. Saralyn was exquisite. David would never dream of looking at another woman if she were his...

He paused and turned to look back at the villa. The plate was empty. His heart was full. He was aware he'd avoided her question last night. It had come as a surprise. And he wasn't good with surprises.

Could they do the dating thing? Having considered it in the quiet dark hours after they'd made love last night, he concluded that he'd like that very much. But how to do that when she lived in California and he in New York? He could fly to see her every weekend. The expense was nothing. But she did have plans to move. Could he entice her to settle in New York City? He'd gotten the impression that she preferred a smaller town, someplace cozy and far from the flash of paparazzi.

His life was generally paparazzi-free. Generally. The trial had shuffled the media out from their caves. There wasn't a day he could walk from his Manhattan penthouse to the coffee shop down the street without encountering one or half a dozen with microphones and recording devices in hand. He'd accepted that his being a billionaire and the owner of Crown Corp attracted media interest. He had no problem with their interest, because he could compartmentalize and set that aside as a work issue. But when they invaded his private life, it made dealing more difficult.

He wanted to return home and have life reset to before the trial. Everything fine. Crown Corp kept producing blankets and his new projects would be on track to begin production. But unless he stepped up and made a decision one way or another on the blanket, it might forever be polluted with the media's opinion and the intense inner turmoil that had settled into his very soul.

That poor child.

Gripping the plate and staring down at it, he shook his head. He'd come here to make a decision. Saralyn was busy working. Now he must focus on how to move forward.

Returning to the chef's cottage, he washed the plate and then grabbed his walking kit—a rucksack fitted with binoculars for bird-watching, scuba mask for diving, and a machete for interesting finds—and set out to the far side of the island opposite from the villa.

Writing through lunch and only coming up for air midafternoon was a writer's dream. Yet Saralyn could no longer ignore her rumbling stomach, so she heated up a delicious shakshuka and devoured it.

Wondering where David had gone, she figured he must be doing work stuff. The CEO of Crown Corp could hardly tuck his phone in a Faraday box. That he'd left her to write had been beyond thoughtful. She hadn't even had to roll her eyes at him!

It was rare that nonwriters understood the writing process. That when the muse struck, she must be followed, entertained, preened over, which meant sitting before the keyboard until your fingers bled. Not literally but metaphorically. Spill it all onto the page. Also, an author could be writing when simply sitting on the sofa, eyelids half-closed. How Saralyn's imagination wandered. And she'd been following it since she was a kid. That she could make a living using her imagination was a blessing.

But writing autobiographies for celebrities did not require imagination. And while the fiction she ghostwrote did require a cooperative muse, it still felt distant from her heart. This historical project flamed in her chest and wanted her attention. The characters were so interesting! It was such an incredible feeling.

Her phone pinged. She'd forgotten to tuck it away in the Faraday box after checking her emails. Her mom had sent birthday wishes and a gift card for Saralyn's favorite cookie shop. Always appreciated, even if one monstrous cookie tended to tip the scales at eight hundred calories.

She glanced to the phone and just caught the notification with her agent's name across the top of the screen. She knew what Leslie was calling for. And while she should ignore it, it was time to face the life-changing decision she'd come here to make. One she had moved toward since arriving.

Pressing the answer button and putting it on speaker, she said "Hi" to Leslie, who immediately sighed and began her spiel about how Saralyn was taking an inordinate amount of time deciding. What was wrong? Was it the divorce? When would she get over that? It was time to move on. She needed this money!

Actually, she had moved on. And she had *gotten over it*. And she didn't need the money as much as her reactionary gut wanted her to believe she did. She had the settlement, which would allow her some financial cushion as she explored her writing options.

It was time to stand on her own two feet and use her own name. To be herself.

"I'm going to pass on this contract." Saralyn felt her confidence rise, yet still her spine tingled with nerves. "It feels right. I've been working on the historical project I mentioned to you last time we talked."

"Saralyn, you can't sell under your own name."

"Why not? New authors sell every day."

She was aware she was contractually bound not to reveal who she wrote for to any publishers. When submitting under a different name, she could only say that she was a ghostwriter. So, yes, this would be like starting over as a new author.

"And I've realized a lot of my fear over trying to make a go under my own name is because Brock kept me in a position of feeling lesser, like I needed him to support me. I've thought about it," she said to Leslie. "I have to do this."

Another heavy sigh. "Well, then, I hate to do this but I believe we have to break ties. I've held up the other author's agent long enough on this. Had her convinced you would take the project. Saralyn, this is easy money. And you know the writer's style and voice so well. Is it the movie potential? I can see if I can get you a piece of the residuals."

That would be a nice bonus, but it wouldn't

go anywhere near giving her the recognition or creative freedom she desired. It was too little, with no regard for her work.

"It's not that. I'm ready for a change. I want to write under my own name."

"Martin isn't even your name."

Writing under her maiden name as Saralyn Hayes suited her. It was just another change that felt right.

"I'm decided, Leslie. And if you feel you can no longer represent me…" She would never get Leslie's full support in representing the new work. The woman had once been a shark in the publishing world; now it seemed she'd slipped into the easy sales with established clients and editors who knew her. "I can accept that. I'm sorry. You've done so much for me over the years." Except the parts about wheedling her into ghostwriting forever and taking the sure jobs. And discouraging her from writing under her own name. "Thank you for everything."

"Saralyn, I can't believe you can walk away from this offer so easily."

"It's not easy. Life hasn't been easy these past few years. But it's turning around." She glanced out at the azure sky, tufted along the edges with emerald palm trees and frosted with white foam wavering back and forth on the pale sands. "I am happy with my decision. Please send me whatever paperwork needs to be done to finalize our working together. Is there anything else?"

A scoff suited Leslie; the woman was abrupt and to the point, sometimes painfully so. She'd get over it. She boasted a client list of many famous names. "You'll never sell," she finally said. "I'll forward the dissolution forms to you."

The phone clicked off. Not even a goodbye.

Saralyn set down the phone and realized her fingers were shaking. She'd done it. She'd taken the step that she hoped would be the right one.

But was it?

Self-doubt crashed against her newly gained courage and she heaved up a stuttering breath that blossomed to tears.

"What have I done?"

CHAPTER FIFTEEN

LAST NIGHT DAVID had returned to the villa to find Saralyn in a quiet mood. She'd said she didn't want to talk, only to make love. So they had, as the sun set and the noises of tropical birds and insects settled for the night. But this morning, David had snuck out of bed and wandered the beach, phone in hand. It was becoming almost impossible to ignore the demands of real life.

Crown Corp needed him. Ryan Wexley, the company's COO called. The press wanted a statement from David. If they didn't get one they planned to go ahead with the "cleared of wrong-doing in trial but still hiding secrets. Do you trust your safety to this man's blanket?" head-line. It was a cruel way to get him to talk. The media had access to the trial transcripts. But David could no longer avoid his responsibilities to the company. A statement was necessary. And not one sent via Zoom or video. It had to be in person. David had to connect with the public through a press conference, Ryan had said.

Ryan transferred David to his secretary. She would book a flight from the mainland to New York and let him know when the boat would arrive to ferry him. Tomorrow, though. He needed one last day with Saralyn.

They'd begun something amazing that he didn't want to walk away from. And she had indicated she'd felt the same. But how to make it work?

He didn't want to throw money at her or put her up in an apartment. That wasn't his style or hers. But was he prepared for what he suspected was her style? A real relationship where the couple lived together, in a real home, with real lives and respect and trust in one another. It sounded like a dream his younger self had chased for so long. He'd finally skidded to the side of the track and sat down, gasping, knowing he'd never reach such an untouchable goal.

The only way he could move forward with Saralyn was to open up completely to her. And he didn't know how to do that.

It was Saralyn who suggested they go sailing. David took her out on the streamlined, small dinghy and when the wind caught the sails, they glided over the turquoise waters. Laughter bubbled up and, in the moment, she didn't think to take notes for her writing. Though now as they floated, the sail barely billowing, and she lying on the bow deck with her chin on her fist, she did make some mental notes on the adventure.

"Writing?" David asked as he joined her and sat near the mast, hand securely on the rope that controlled the wheel.

"I'm not always writing when I'm quiet," she protested.

"Liar."

"Fine. You win. I can't *not* make notes about new experiences. And this one was exhilarating. But the wind has died down. How will we get back to shore?"

They were about a quarter mile from the beach and the wind had disappeared.

"It'll pick up. And if not, we've got paddles stashed right there." He kicked the side of the boat. "In fact, we're going the paddle route to get back. More research for you, eh? That'll build your swimming muscles."

"I'm up for it." She turned to her side and flipped a hank of hair over her shoulder. "I got a call from my agent yesterday. It's…well, it's why I didn't want to talk much last night."

"I understand. Sometimes sex is better than words."

"I completely agree. But now I need to talk about it. My agent was not happy. Make that my former agent."

"What went down?"

"I told her I wasn't going to write the next ghost book. I want to focus on my own stuff now."

"I'm proud of you."

"Yes. Well." She rolled to her back and spread out her arms across the fiberglass deck. The sun warmed her skin like a lover's caress. "Did I do the right thing? I'm having second thoughts, David. What have I done?"

"Sounds like you've become Saralyn Hayes."

Closing her eyes, she smiled at that statement. He got her. What a thrill to be involved with a man who could see into her, interpret her and get it right. It was almost as thrilling as making love with him. And yet that ingrained part of her that sought safety and security niggled.

"I could have taken one last job. Used that money to live on while I search for a place to put down some roots."

"You don't have any savings?"

"The divorce settlement gave me enough that I don't need an immediate income, but… It's my survivor mentality. Hard to shake."

He leaned over her and kissed her. Long, slow, delicious. Rocking on some sudden waves, their bodies brushed, caressed, and glided sensually. "You did the right thing, Saralyn. Don't question it. You followed your heart. Now all you have to do is keep following it."

"You make me believe I can do anything."

"Why can't you?"

"Selling under a new name will be the challenge."

"If the writing you've done for another author ended up on the silver screen I'm going to guess you're a damned excellent writer. You'll find your groove."

She stroked her fingers alongside his face. "I have found it. Now I need to groove on into a nice little place to write while I'm moving. My mom offered to let me stay with her, but that's a big no."

"You and your mom don't get along?"

"I adore my mother. She's a hippie who never grew out of her macramé sweater and hip-hugging jeans. She's an entrepreneur. She sells essential oils, yoga stuff and little witchy spells online. Makes some good money doing it."

"She sounds interesting."

"And…she's got a boyfriend who adores her. At seventy-five years old, my mother is getting it more than I am."

"Wait a minute—"

"My mom *was* getting it more than me," she quickly corrected.

"I wouldn't want you to feel inferior to your mother. Now, are you ready to paddle?"

She slid her hand down his chest and to his swim trunks. "First…"

He waggled a brow at her. "Out here?"

"Not up for it, lover?"

"I am up for anything and everything as long as it's with you."

CHAPTER SIXTEEN

AFTER A LIFE-CHANGING filet mignon that had melted on her tongue, Saralyn had taken charge of the dishes. David had gotten yet another phone call and wandered out to the beach while talking. Setting the last dried dish in the cupboard, she wrapped the gauzy floral scarf about her hips and wandered outside.

She spied David sitting on one of the swings amid the turquoise water. Evening sun glimmered in silver slashes on the surface. He wasn't swinging. Just sitting there. First glance, she sensed he was thinking and decided to give him his space.

Yet her heart wouldn't allow her to walk by him. Once again, she had to remind herself that it wasn't all about her. This island was a refuge for tattered souls. And as far as she knew, David's soul was still torn around the edges. Had he solved the dilemma he'd come here to work on? The man was hurting, and she couldn't dismiss that. She cared about him. And he needed to know that. Because it seemed all his life he'd wondered if anyone did care about him. That his parents had been so distant crushed her. Thanks to a thoughtful chef employed in his childhood home he'd grown into a kind man who did so much for so many, but she knew deep inside he craved the attention he'd never been given.

"Just like me," she realized with new wonder.

They were two alike. Yet, the more she grew to know David, the less and less she desired attention. Fame. *Being noticed.* Yes, she wanted to write under her own name. But she didn't really want the spotlight or adulation. That felt like ego and so surface. Something was altering in her. Scales were tilting and finding a new balance. He had done that for her.

Wading into the water, she sloshed a little to alert him that she approached. "Okay if I join you?"

He nodded and tucked the wallet he'd been holding into his shirt pocket. Then he tilted his head against one of the swing ropes that suspended it from the framework.

Still he didn't face her. And he didn't say much more.

Saralyn slid onto the swing and tickled her toes across the water's surface. The man owned this island. He was a billionaire. He had everything he could ever desire. Save for an ineffable something she suspected could only come from within.

"Want to talk about it?" she tried. "Or is this one of those let's-be-quiet moments?"

He smirked. "I've been sitting here awhile so I've reached maximum quiet mode. I don't mind talking, especially to you. I need to talk. But it's heavy."

"Is it about the reason you fled here? Getting away from media and the lawsuit?"

"You really don't know about the lawsuit?"

More than ever, she wished she'd remembered to research him online so she could relate to what he was going through and perhaps make it easier for him so he wouldn't have to explain, but... "Sorry, but I don't. I only check in with the news about once a month."

"You are an anomaly. I can't believe you were married to an actor for so long and yet managed to avoid the press and news."

"It's a habit I developed over the years. After the divorce, I grew vigilant about it. Not being on social media helps a lot. And as a ghostwriter, I don't have to worry about putting on a public face and talking to fans online."

She reached out and slid her fingertips along his thigh, but he didn't make a move to hold her hand.

"Before I get into what's bugging me, I want

to ask you something." He absently patted his shirt pocket. "Do you have children?"

"No."

"Do you want to have children?"

She chuckled softly. "Honestly? Yes, I did once. I had dreams of domesticity. But Brock didn't. So my dreams changed. Over the years, I realized I enjoy children, but I much prefer not having to care for them. As for having them now? Remember—" she splayed out her arms in dramatic declaration "—*menopause*! So even if I did feel the tug to procreate I'd be tough out of luck."

"Oh. Sure. Sorry, I didn't mean to intrude into your personal stuff."

"I think we've moved beyond the personal intrusion stage. Menopause isn't the big scary. The hot flashes are rare. I put on an extra ten pounds. I'm dealing. And I can have sex without contraception. That's a bonus, especially when my sexy younger lover is so demanding."

His smile was soft but genuine.

"But honestly, having a child. In my house. Twenty-four/seven. Having to mold them, teach them, protect them?" She sighed. "It's a huge job. I can barely take care of myself some days. What about you?"

"Me? Having kids?"

She nodded.

"I'm on the same page as you are. I love children but I wouldn't know how to take care of them. My parents didn't offer exemplary role models to learn from. I'd never want to raise a child in such an awkward distant relationship such as I experienced." He sighed heavily and took the wallet out from his pocket. He didn't open it. Just tapped it against his thigh. "I can't stop thinking about how children have no power or control over what the adults in their lives do with them. It's very sad. Because of that... I've decided to stop production on the blanket."

So that was what he'd come here to make a decision about? But he was stopping production on the blanket because...of his childhood? "Oh, David, that's...a huge decision."

"It is. The lawsuit was brought against Crown Corp," he said. "It was a wrongful-death suit."

She hadn't expected— Well, she hadn't conjured any expectation. "Oh."

He opened the wallet, pulled out a photograph and handed it to her without saying anything. It was a boy, perhaps five or six, smiling brightly to reveal a missing front tooth. His blond hair was tousled. His cheeks freckled. A relative? Someone he knew?

"This is what happened." David shifted on the swing but didn't turn to face her. "Crown Corp was charged in the death of that six-year-old boy you are looking at right now. Which comes down to me, personally. The plaintiffs stated the blanket had literally squeezed their child to death." He did turn his head to catch her open-mouthed and truly aghast. "That's impossible. We've had the blankets tested, certified. There's no possibility it could ever exert more than .010 of pressure. Like touching a baby's skin with a gentle nudge. I never would have put the blanket into production if there had been an inkling of a chance it could cause harm."

Saralyn held the photo carefully. The boy's smile hit her differently now. Right in the gut. "Then, how did it happen?"

David scrubbed his fingers back through his hair. Bit his lip. His knee bounced lightly, creating waves in the water around his calves.

"I attended the trial every day. It went on for weeks. The plaintiff's lawyers were tough. Really knew how to tell a story. Appeal to the jury. I almost began to believe I *did* have a hand in the boy's death. But the coroner's reports told a very clear story. The child had fallen down a full run of metal-edged stairs. The impact killed him instantly. He'd landed on the blanket. The parents were…outside at the time. They didn't even hear him scream.

"An expert coroner confirmed a contusion to the head was the killing blow. The parents had genuinely believed he'd been wrapped in the blanket and it had caused the death, but as the coroner's details were revealed, they accepted the truth."

Saralyn's entire body had tightened to a tense knot. How awful!

"The jury found Crown Corp not guilty of any involvement in the boy's death. And blessedly, the judge dismissed a negligence charge against the parents."

The heavy breath that exited David filled the air with a sadness Saralyn could feel. He held out his hand and she placed the photo on it.

"His name was Charlie," he said. "I will never forget him. Ever."

Tucking the photo away, he lifted his shoulders. And when he gasped a shuddering breath and then sniffed, Saralyn couldn't bear it. She stepped off the swing and walked around in front of him. He looked up to her, tears in his eyes. Just before she said, "it's not the blanket's fault, you were cleared" she stopped herself. No words could erase the ugly pain that had been inflicted on that child, the family and, inadvertently, David.

"I can't imagine how terrible you must feel for that family," she said. "For that child. Keeping his picture with you is a lovely way to honor him."

Shaking his head and bowing it, his shoulders

dropped. A deep emotion pushed up from his depths. The air between them grew heavy and it tugged at her heart. Her soul leaned forward, seeking his. Her body followed. She touched his arm and, with her other hand, caressed his jaw.

"I will always feel responsible," he managed.

"No, you mustn't. Oh, David."

"Logically, I know it wasn't the blanket," he said. "It was actually there to…cushion his landing. Not enough, though." He inhaled heavily. "Crown Corp was cleared of any wrongdoing. But I'm haunted by the trial. I was meant to be there. To stand as a witness for that child's unfortunate death. Saralyn, I have to pull the plug on the blanket. I can't put it out in public anymore. It's…tainted. Wrong."

While she knew the blanket was not at all tainted, she could have no idea what the media and consumers thought of it. Truly, she hadn't seen anything on the little news she'd watched. But there must have been a media sensation in New York City. Certainly, initially, David and his company may have been accused. Emotionally, he must have been a wreck.

"It feels like the right thing to do." His body shuddered minutely. "And yet, is it? I don't know. I thought I'd come here to find the answer. I've been so busy with…"

With her? Oh. That hurt her heart. And yet, if

she had distracted him from those wretched feelings for a little while, she wanted to claim that as a victory. But that triumph felt selfish. This was about him. And while she didn't know how to help him with this pain, she could be there for him.

Saralyn wrapped her arms over his shoulders and bowed her head to the side of his. "I can't tell you what to do in this situation. But I can be here for you." She hugged against him, standing between his legs and fitting her body into an embrace that she sensed would make him skittish. No way not to do it, though. The compulsion felt right. "You can tell me anything, anytime," she added. "And you can let it out. I've got you."

And in that moment, his body melded against hers and his arms wrapped across her back. He pulled her in tightly, burying his face against her shoulder and hair. And he sobbed quietly.

The man had been witness to something terrible, but as he'd said, perhaps he'd been meant to be at that trial, to bear witness in the child's name. And as she pulled him in closer, so deeply she wanted to crush his soul against hers, tears fell down Saralyn's cheeks. David was that boy. Not given physical affection as a child and fighting his own way through the world, navigating it well, but ultimately, ever seeking.

When he pulled back and gave one of those

self-conscious laughs people do when they've just exposed a private part of themselves, Saralyn brushed the hair from his cheek and kissed his forehead. "I care about you, David. Thank you for telling me that. I know it was difficult."

"I trust you. I feel safe in your arms. I…I just let you hug me," he said in a wondrous tone.

She nodded. "You did. And you can have another whenever you desire."

"Like…" He studied their loose embrace, marveling over the surprise of it. A smile overtook his sadness. "Right now…?"

"Most definitely."

Their embrace resumed. He held her close, easily yet firmly. If he never let her go, she would live with that. He could take whatever he needed from her. It was easy to give what she could to one she cared for so deeply.

"So this is a hug," he whispered, and gave her a quick, tight squeeze before loosening to hold her gently. "It wasn't so difficult as I imagined."

"I think because it came to you at the moment you needed it most." She kissed his forehead and pushed away the hair from his eye. Her lovely man. Her precious hero who sought only to protect the innocent. "I know I just said I couldn't tell you what to do, but I do need to state what I believe. That blanket has helped so many people, David. It would be a shame if you were to cease its production. Maybe you should let the public decide if it's something they want?"

"I don't understand?"

"I've seen big corporations apologize to the public and then they allow consumers to either continue to purchase the product or not. If it fails, that's your answer. If it continues to sell, that means people still need it."

"A public apology. Yes, I need to do that. My lawyers said I shouldn't. That I should just ignore it and it would go away."

"That's lawyers for you. But I know you. And this pain eating away at you won't truly go away until you release it."

"My COO called again this morning. The press is chomping at the bit for a statement from me, and they've threatened to go with some damning headlines if I don't speak to them. In person."

"Maybe an apology might be the thing that helps you?"

He kissed her hand and pressed his cheek against her chest, holding her firmly. "You're very smart, Saralyn. Thank you."

She bowed her head to his and caressed his body against hers. It felt right to give him what he needed and she prayed that he could rise above the torment that haunted his soul. Strong, smart and empathetic, he most surely would.

CHAPTER SEVENTEEN

A WARM QUICHE sat on the table, along with a pitcher of sangria and a tropical flower stuck in a tiny vase near the single plate.

Saralyn frowned. She'd been in the shower, luxuriating under the hot stream for longer than usual. And in that time, David had made breakfast and then…disappeared. She scanned through all the windows and open doorways and didn't see him on the veranda. After they'd made love last night, he'd reminded her he needed to return to New York to make a statement. Surely, she wouldn't leave without saying goodbye to her—

Oh! Whew! There he was, walking on the beach. Talking to someone on the phone.

She sat and dished up a serving of quiche and sipped the sangria. "Wherever I land when I go back to the States I most definitely will always have sangria in my home."

It would remind her of this dreamy vacation, the warm tropical breezes and bright turquoise waters. And that a man she cared deeply for had been so kind to think of her before he returned to business duties.

It was more than that. Saralyn put down her fork and caught her chin in hand as she watched David pace in the distance, his arm gesturing as he spoke words she couldn't hear. Swim trunks again this morning, and nothing else. He was an island man and could exist in trunks and bare feet if he had no pressing concerns or work to tend. He was so rich he could do just that. But his inventive nature and caring heart wouldn't allow him to sit back and get fat off his riches. She loved that about him. He cared so much the death of a child had cracked his heart and now made him question everything.

Perhaps he cared too much.

She didn't want him to stop producing the blanket. It helped so many and could continue to do so. But he had to come to terms with the whole lawsuit and the boy's horrendous death before he could move forward.

"I wish I could hold your hand and walk you through it," she said. "I love you."

Saralyn sat straight. The words had come out of her mouth. She hadn't thought about them; it had been a true and honest statement.

"I really do love him." Her heart had taken a wild ride these past days.

Could they do the couple thing?

"He's not *that* young," she reasoned now as

she finished the quiche. "He's smart and responsible."

And it wasn't as though she were dating a man in his twenties. A youngster barely out of college and just finding his way in the world of business, career and family. A man who may be uncertain about his future and may look to an older woman for guidance. David Crown was her equal in most every way. Her charming hero and daring rescuer. Her quiet conversationalist. Her lover. Her confidante. Her backup musician in the Galaxy Lounge.

He made her feel like Miss Stardust, standing before an audience, milking the attention and thriving in it. And if she never sold another book, never made a name for herself and readers began to know her by her real name, she could care little. Because in David's eyes, she was a star.

He'd told her to remember how exquisite she was.

Yes, she was.

Dare she tell him she loved him?

"Why not?" she whispered. "This is my new chapter. It's time to live it. Take a chance, Miss Stardust. The worst he can do is reject you."

She'd hate that. But it would be another lesson learned.

She shook her head. No, rejection would gut her. She couldn't endure another man shoving her aside as if she had limited use.

"I can't risk it." Maybe?

Downing the sangria in one long swallow, she set down the glass. It wasn't the heavy alcohol content of the drink that made her nod her head. It was the new and improved Saralyn Hayes who bravely stood and decided to take what she wanted.

The moment her feet hit the veranda, David turned and jogged toward her.

"Now or never," she whispered. She had to tell him she loved him. From there, they'd figure things out.

"Just got a call from the office." He stepped onto the veranda and shook the sand from his bare feet. "The boat will be here in an hour to pick me up. PR is working on a speech they want me to give to the press this afternoon."

"A speech?" This afternoon was…but hours away.

He wandered over and kissed her. "Mmm, sangria." With a brush of his hands through her hair, he slid them down to her shoulders and eyed her carefully. "I told you last night I had to leave."

"Right."

Had she been ready to tell him something? It didn't matter now. The man was leaving. He had important business to tend. And what did it matter if a silly writer had fallen in love with him and wanted to spend the rest of her days with him?

"You need to go. But David." She clasped his

hand and squeezed. "You're not seriously going to stop production of the blanket, are you?"

He sighed heavily. "I honestly can't say. It's going to be foremost in my thoughts the entire flight home." He kissed her quickly on the forehead. "I have to gather my things. I'll be back so we can say goodbye!" He took off across the beach for the chef's cottage, waving as he did.

Saralyn's wave wilted faster than did her heart. Because her heart was doing a slow melt and sat jiggling in her ribcage.

So this was how it would end?

A tear slipped down her cheek.

David gathered the few items of clothing he'd brought to the island and shoved them in a duffel bag. No shoes. Those would be waiting for him on the pickup boat. A few toiletries. His laptop and phone. He wandered through the cottage, closing windows and turning off any electrical devices. A cleanup crew would arrive after Saralyn left the island, but he could never leave the place a mess.

He grabbed his duffel and stepped outside, pulling the door shut behind him. He'd donned a shirt but still wore his swim trunks. He'd change on the jet. When he arrived at JFK airport he'd head immediately to work. They were waiting for him to go over the speech. Media outlets had been invited to the press briefing.

This was all happening quickly. And while he was a master at shifting modes and tasks this was *the big one*. The one where he must put his heart out there for all to see. It was not going to be easy. He'd only just summoned the courage to reveal that part of his heart to one woman. And now to do it before the world?

He wished Saralyn could be there to hold his hand. Give him the hug he'd learned how to accept from her kind and comforting embrace.

"Saralyn," he muttered.

Was he to dash off and leave her behind? What kind of idiot was he? No fool would leave such a woman behind. Especially since she'd recently taken ownership of his heart. Shaun had called it. Love had snuck up on him.

Did he have time to fall to his knees and profess his undying love to Saralyn? It would feel rushed, disingenuous. And he knew if he attempted such a ruse she would feel that forced emotion. But there were no dragons to be slain in the half hour before his ride arrived. No way to win the heroine's heart.

How to do this and not lose the girl?

He didn't know how to tell a woman he loved her. He'd never done it before. Could he tap into that emotion while also focusing on the afternoon's important press conference? He was feeling everything right now. It was starting to blur and make him feel unsure.

No. He thrived on the challenge of juggling multiple tasks at work. Adding in a personal life task?

He picked up the duffle and started to walk. "You've got this, Crown. Go win the girl."

Never in his life had he felt more purposeful or determined. Not even the initial release of the hug blanket had set such a fire beneath his feet. He was going to win the girl!

Taking the walk to the villa swiftly, sand flew in his wake and the birds cawed as if cheering him on. He turned around the last palm tree before the beach and almost crashed right into Saralyn.

She stepped back with a big smile on her face and announced, "David!"

"Saralyn?" He eyed the suitcase at her side. "I was just…"

"I'm coming with you," she stated. "I know I have a few days left on my stay, but I won't take no for an answer. I want to be there for you when you tell the world how you stand behind your product. And when you step back from the podium and turn around, I'll give you the biggest and best hug ever. Because… David, I love you."

Mouth open in shock, David nodded. And then his smile burst and he pulled her into an embrace and spun her. Their laughter echoed. And their embrace turned into a long and soul-touching hug.

"I love you," he said to her. "So you'll come to New York with me? I…can't believe this is happening. I didn't even have to slay any dragons."

She quirked a brow.

"I was headed here to win you over. To slay the dragon and take you home with me."

"You did help me slay a dragon or two. I would never have had the confidence to invite myself into your life if it hadn't been for the love, kindness and respect you've shown me since I set foot on this island. Can we make this work?"

"It's already working." He kissed her. "You're my girl, Saralyn."

"And you are my knight in a soft blanket cape."

He made a superhero pose, arms stretched out as if flying, then snapped his arms to a muscle-pumping pose.

Saralyn's laugh filled the air. "My hero!"

He picked up her suitcase. Across the beach the pickup boat slowly glided up to dock. "Let's do this."

"Right behind you, lover."

He stopped and shook his head. "I don't want you behind me. I want you beside me, Saralyn."

A tear spilled down her cheek and slipped into her smile. "David Crown, I love you."

EPILOGUE

DAVID'S SPEECH TO the press went well. He spoke from the heart, explaining the details from the trial that were not too exploitative to put out to the public. And while he knew the blanket had not caused the death, he felt the immense responsibility for the safety of children. Crown Corp would continue to produce the blanket—all proceeds would go to Charlie's Care, a charity he would create to foot hospital bills for uninsured children.

When he'd stepped away from the press stand, he turned and walked right into Saralyn's arms. Their hug drowned out the cacophony of the camera flashes and shouting journalists. Saralyn could only feel David's heartbeat against hers.

And when finally David turned to answer the one question repeated most: "Who is she?" he'd answered with a smiling, "She's my girlfriend, Saralyn Hayes, a writer you'll want to read, and we're in love."

Days later, after a tour of Crown Corp, a few nights treated to the rich and luxurious five-star restaurants in New York City, and a leisurely afternoon spent strolling through Central Park, Saralyn sat on the floor of David's thirty-second floor penthouse that overlooked the massive city park. The two corner walls of the living room were floor-to-ceiling windows, and the city lights dazzled while they snuggled with a blanket and listened to Frank Sinatra crooning over the speakers.

The wine was chilled, the recently delivered Midnight Munchies cookies had been eaten, and they'd made love for the second time that day. Naked and giggling as they arranged themselves beneath the giant hug blanket, Saralyn sighed as the blanket embraced them gently.

"This is so amazing," she said. "But I like your hugs better."

"I intend to practice the fine art of hugging as much as possible. If that's okay with you?"

"Practice on me all you like. So what's up next for Crown Corp? You mentioned you're announcing a new product soon?"

"Yes, it's the Body Tuner. It's worn across the shoulders and resonates a healing frequency throughout the body. I'm hoping it'll be bigger than the blanket. And maybe it'll help erase some of the sadness I feel whenever I think about that boy."

"You're grieving, David. Don't rush it. Just go

with the feelings. And the charity you've created is such a perfect way to honor Charlie. I love that the child has a kind heart to think about him."

"I could never stop thinking about him. Do you think the new product will be a good thing?"

"I know the power of resonate-frequency healing is real. And with you behind it, it'll conquer the world."

"Will you be by my side to watch that conquest?"

"If you'll have me. Though…" She winced and looked aside.

All was well. And yet, now that David had conquered his immediate emotional threats, she still had a few of her own. She intended to contact a Realtor to look for a home, but she still wasn't sure where she wanted to plant roots. David had already asked her to stay in New York with him. It felt…

"Plotting?" he asked.

She turned back and kissed him. "Thinking about where I'm going to land and when I'll find the time to finish the story I've decided to write."

"I kind of thought you'd stay here with me. You can get a lot of writing done while I'm at work."

"I could, and honestly? I don't want to leave you. But. I don't know. And please don't take this the wrong way, but New York doesn't feel quite right. It's big and bustling. Like Los Angeles was."

"I get it."

"You do?"

"I do. And here's how much I get it. While you're figuring out where to land with a forever home, what about packing up your laptop and taking your muse to Greece to write the story?"

Saralyn pressed both her hands to his cheeks to study his gaze. The man was dead serious. And those deep brown eyes never lied to her. "Greece?"

"Yes, it's a country in the Mediterranean."

"I know where Greece is, you teaser. But what do you mean? Another island adventure but this time to write? I'm not sure that's in my budget. I feel like I need to pay Juliane for the trip. It wasn't cheap."

"Your friend's credit charge has been refunded."

"What?"

He shrugged. "I wanted to do that for you. And for a friend who is so good to you that she gave you such a generous trip."

"Oh, David, that's too kind of you." She kissed him. "Thank you. Juliane will be so happy to hear that."

"As for paying for a trip to Greece, I'll let you pick up the airfare, strong independent woman that you are, but the stay is on me. I own a place in Mykonos. It's my winter home. I like to spend time there when I've ideas to brew in my brain. Prelab ideas that usually barrel out of my gray matter like confetti bursting in a party. Would you accept?"

"A free stay in Greece? To write?"

But it was too generous. And what would he expect in return? Did she want to be beholden to another man?

No, she mustn't view it in such a manner. It was a gift, offered without strings, as only David Crown could do.

"What Mediterranean adventure is taking place inside that beautiful brain of yours right now?"

"The adventure of having all the time in the world to focus on a project that means the world to me. How long could I stay?"

"As long as you desire. And you should invite your mom and her boyfriend for a week or two. Of course, I did say it's my winter home. I may stop in in a few months."

"I'd be disappointed if you did not."

His smile grew. "Does that mean you'll accept?"

She nodded. "I'm no fool. The bustle of Manhattan offers nothing over blue waters and white sands."

"Fair enough. Would it be okay if I flew in to stay with you every weekend?"

"I'd be upset if you did not, lover. My mom will be over the moon for the trip."

"I'd love to meet her. And her boyfriend."

"Will I ever meet your parents?"

"Do you want to?"

"I do. I want us to be…family."

"Yeah? I like the sound of that."

"Really?"

"Really. I know we're taking it slow, but I can't imagine going slow with anyone else. Ever." He kissed her deeply against the backdrop of the brightly lit cityscape and they snuggled into the best and longest hug, which segued into passionate lovemaking.

Saralyn had found her groove. And the courage to start anew. And the common sense to confirm she wanted a man in her life. A companion to adventure with, dance with, kiss and laugh with. Would they marry? At the moment, it wasn't important. Simply being in love was an out-of-this-world experience the twosome would embrace and enjoy.

The Galaxy Lounge was now featuring the indomitable Miss Stardust accompanied by her warmhearted, sexy and huggable synth player.

* * * * *

If you enjoyed this story,
check out these other great reads
from Michele Renae

Consequence of Their Parisian Night
Cinderella's Billion-Dollar Invitation
Parisian Escape with the Billionaire
The CEO and the Single Dad

All available now!

HARLEQUIN
Reader Service

Enjoyed your book?

Try the perfect subscription for Romance readers and get more great books like this delivered right to your door.

See why over 10+ million readers have tried Harlequin Reader Service.

Start with a Free Welcome Collection with free books and a gift—valued over $20.

Choose any series in print or ebook. See website for details and order today:

TryReaderService.com/subscriptions

RSBPA24R